The Cure for Disgruntlement

By the Same Author

Novels
The Restraint of Beasts
All Quiet on the Orient Express
Three to See the King
The Scheme for Full Employment
Explorers of the New Century
The Maintenance of Headway
A Cruel Bird Came to the Nest and Looked In
The Field of the Cloth of Gold
The Forensic Records Society
Tales of Muffled Oars
The Trouble with Sunbathers
Sunbathers in a Bottle
Mistaken for Sunbathers

Stories
Once in a Blue Moon
Only When the Sun Shines Brightly
Screwtop Thompson and Other Tales

The Cure for Disgruntlement

Magnus Mills

QUOQS

Quoqs Publishing for Magnus Mills

First Published 2023

Kindle Direct Publishing

This book is work of a fiction. The names and characters are from the author's imagination and any resemblance to actual persons living or dead, is entirely coincidental.

No part of this publication may be reproduced in any form or means without prior written permission from the publisher.

Cover designed by Quoqs

Cover illustration by iStock\Nikada

Copyright © Magnus Mills 2023

10 9 8 7 6 5 4 3 2

All rights reserved.

For Sue

1

We arrived by sea, of course, because in those days it was the only way to travel. Our preparations were thorough: we'd brought all our own provisions as well as maps, charts and reference books. We had no wish to impinge on our hosts in any way. We also went to great lengths to take account of their feelings. We knew they weren't expecting us so we waited until it was broad daylight before we approached the shore. This would signal that our intentions were honourable and that there'd be no question of us trying to sneak in while their backs were turned. We were certain they would understand. Once we'd beached our boat we took care not to stray very far inland. We didn't want them to think we were encroaching too much. We moved into the shelter of a breakwater and began erecting the tents.

'Should be alright here as long as we keep the place tidy,' said Harcourt. 'Tidiness is their most important tradition.'

Beyond the beach the seafront was lined with three-storey buildings standing side-by-side and each painted a different colour. One or two faces appeared at their windows as we settled in but they withdrew again when they saw us looking. The beach itself was deserted. A distant clock struck nine.

'Do you think they'll send somebody to welcome us?' I asked.

'I should imagine so,' Harcourt replied. 'It is customary, after all.'

'In the meantime I'll get breakfast ready.'

'Right.'

I unpacked the hamper while Harcourt and the others wandered along the beach in search of driftwood for a fire. By now a few people had emerged from the buildings and were walking along the seafront. The majority seemed to be in a great hurry to get wherever they were going but plainly there were some who had a bit more time on their hands. Eventually two of them stopped to greet one another, then they came to the railings and stood talking. They took little notice of the activity below them and instead cast an occasional glance towards the sea. This suggested they were merely discussing the weather. When enough driftwood had been gathered Harcourt returned and quickly got a fire going.

'We'll need fresh water,' said Kingsnorth.

He went off with a container to find some.

'I spotted a public shower at the top of the beach,' said Harcourt. 'There'll probably be a handy tap nearby. I understand these facilities are provided along the full length of the coastline.'

'Another feather in their collective cap,' I remarked.

We'd been highly impressed by what we'd heard about the achievements of these people. Their civilisation was apparently developed to a high degree of sophistication and virtually every contingency had been thought of. They were prosperous too. Nothing was wanting in this land of plenty where almost every amenity was more or less taken for granted. We'd also learnt, however, that for some reason they weren't entirely happy. Apart from a few notable exceptions they seemingly all lived in a state of gloom and despondency. Nobody had been able to explain to us the precise cause of their perpetual melancholy. Nor could anybody offer a plausible solution. We'd received this news with alarm and it had been the source of much conjecture amongst my companions and me. Although the general conclusion was that the inhabitants were beyond help a small group of us had decided that we should at least try. Perhaps if we worked our way into the midst of these forlorn people we might get to know them a little better. Possibly even find some answers and free them from their malaise. With this in mind we'd assembled our expedition and set off across the sea. Harcourt considered himself to be our leader but actually it was a joint venture: we all felt we had something to contribute. Our optimism drove us through the waves and within less than a week we'd made landfall at this pleasant beach.

2

Kingsnorth soon returned with some water and we put the kettle on. We'd heard they were a nation of tea drinkers. Accordingly we'd decided beforehand that our assimilation would be swifter if we all drank tea while we were here (again we'd made sure to bring along an abundant supply).

Oddly enough, though, Kingsnorth reported that he'd seen quite a few people marching along the seafront carrying cups of coffee.

'They didn't stop to drink in the normal leisurely manner you might expect,' he said. 'Instead, they had lids on their cups and went striding past as if there wasn't a minute to spare.'

'Well, they are noted for their punctuality,' said Harcourt. 'We can only assume they wanted to avoid being late.'

'Perhaps they drink tea later in the day,' I ventured.

'Yes, perhaps,' he agreed. 'These details are actually rather important.'

Kingsnorth informed us that he'd noticed a stack of deckchairs at the foot of a stone stairway further along the beach.

'It'll be nice to sit down and stretch the legs after our long voyage,' he added. 'I'll go and fetch some over.'

Johnson accompanied him while Harcourt and I continued preparing breakfast. It was a mild day for the time of year, fairly cloudy, with the sun making occasional appearances. By this time there were several people strolling along the beach, including a man throwing a stick for a dog. The tide was going out so he was able to skirt the end of the breakwater on the seaward side. He passed quite close to our makeshift camp and I tried to catch his eye as he went by. I intended to give him a friendly nod or maybe even a smile and a wave but actually he gave no indication of having seen me. Evidently our presence was of little concern to him.

Breakfast was almost ready when Kingsnorth and Johnson returned with the deckchairs. These were green with white stripes. We placed them in a semicircle before sitting down to eat. Afterwards we spent an agreeable half hour simply taking in our surroundings.

'Fire's a bit smoky,' said Harcourt. 'That driftwood must be damper than it looks.'

'Well, at least they know we're here now,' I replied. 'The smoke's drifting inland. They can't possibly not see it.'

'I think they've known we're here from the very start.'

'They're still keeping their distance nonetheless.'

Harcourt poked the fire.

'Give them time,' he said, 'and I'm sure they'll be less standoffish.'

'As a matter of fact there's somebody coming now,' said Johnson.

A man in a brown linen coat was heading towards us across the sand. He had a purposeful look about him and was carrying some kind of book. As he drew near Harcourt rose to meet him.

'Good morning,' he said.

'Morning,' answered the man. 'You're not supposed to take away the deckchairs until I've booked them out.'

'Ah. Sorry, we didn't realise.'

'Never mind. It's sixpence a day.'

'Oh, er, right.'

'Each.'

Harcourt drew a deep breath.

'Sorry again,' he said, 'but we haven't brought any money with us.'

'Why on earth not?' enquired the man.

'We didn't think it was necessary.'

'We're to help,' I added. 'Voluntarily. There's no mercenary element.'

A look of utter bafflement crossed the man's face. He glanced at the book which now lay open in his hand. It was a book of pink tickets.

'So you're not going to pay,' he said.

'We can return the deckchairs if you like,' offered Harcourt.

'Too late for that,' came the reply. 'Once they've left my safekeeping they count as being hired for the day.'

'But there's hardly any great demand for them,' said Kingsnorth. 'The beach is practically empty.'

'What's that got to do with it?'

'Well, it's not as though we're depriving anyone.'

'Makes no difference,' said the man. 'I'm afraid I'll have to make a report. Can one of you come with me please?'

'Yes, of course,' said Harcourt in a resigned tone of voice.

He appeared rather disheartened so I decided to intervene.

'I'll go,' I said, swiftly rising to my feet. 'Where are we heading?'

'Along to my hut,' said the man.

I could now see that there was a badge pinned to his lapel bearing the words DECKCHAIR ATTENDANT. Together we trudged across the sand to the foot of the stone stairway and up the steps. At the top overlooking the beach was a wooden hut painted entirely green except for a white window frame. He unlocked the door, went inside and closed it. A moment later the window swung open to reveal him perched on a stool behind a counter. Lying before him was another book. This had a red cover labelled DECKCHAIR REPORTS (VARIOUS). He opened it on the first page and upside down I read the printed caption DAMAGE THROUGH NEGLIGENCE. He sighed and shook his head and then leafed through three or four more pages. Eventually he reached the second section which was inscribed WILFUL DAMAGE. A third part was entitled EXCESS BORROWING PERIOD but it seemed he still hadn't found what he was searching for. After turning several more pages he came at last to UNAUTHORISED REMOVAL. He then paused and fixed me with a significant look.

'I'm afraid there'll be a fine to pay,' he announced.

I watched as he wrote a few sentences on the left-hand page. Also the time and date. Then he turned the book towards me, offered me his pen and showed me where to sign. As I did so I noticed that his name was Mr Alder. Lastly he tore off a counterfoil and handed it to me. Apparently we were being fined half a crown.

'Complete waste of time, of course,' he murmured, 'seeing as it's never going to be paid.'

'What makes you think that?' I asked.

I was feeling somewhat affronted.

'Because you people never pay your dues,' he said. 'You come here and take advantage and then we have to pick up the bill.'

'But we haven't come to take advantage,' I protested. 'We've come to help.'

For a few moments he peered at me curiously.

'Oh, yes,' he said at length. 'You mentioned that before.'

'Well, it's true.'

On hearing these words he gave me a further enquiring gaze. Up until now his manner had been rather stern but all of a sudden he appeared to soften a little. He lowered his voice.

'The matter's out of my hands now that I've issued the fine,' he said, 'but take my advice and get it paid as soon as possible. The governors takes a dim view of anybody interfering with the deckchairs.'

'I'll do my best,' I said.

I was about to depart when I was struck by a spark of inspiration.

'Like a cup of tea?' I asked. 'We've just made some fresh.'

'No, thanks all the same,' he replied. 'I've got facilities here for making tea. I've got a fridge as well.'

'There's also some cake,' I added.

I could see him wavering. He looked beyond me towards the broad open expanse of the beach. There was scarcely anyone around.

'Alright, then,' he said. 'I suppose I can spare ten minutes.'

With that he closed the window, emerged from the hut and turned to lock the door. This only took a few seconds but as I waited I noticed a large sign nearby that said NO DOGS ALLOWED ON THE BEACH. Instantly I thought of the man I'd seen throwing sticks for his dog only half an hour ago. It was highly tempting to ask Mr Alder if wrongdoers were fined for such offences. Furthermore, I wondered whether the governors took an equally 'dim view' of them as they did of people who interfered with the deckchairs. In the circumstances, however, I felt it wise to avoid questioning the fairness of their rules. After all this was our first contact with the host nation, so to speak, and it would be a shame to jeopardise it over some quibble. Instead, I led the way down the stone staircase and the pair of us ambled across the beach.

I thought Harcourt looked a little wary as we drew near so I gave him a surreptitious nod before introducing Mr Alder to him and the others. It so happened that the tea we'd made earlier had all been drunk but Kingsnorth quickly set about making some more. I wasn't sure if I should offer our guest a deckchair but in the event it was unnecessary. He sat down on a concrete buttress and quietly consumed his slice of cake. He appeared to have a few misgivings about the fire we'd built until we assured him that it would all be cleared away prior to our departure.

'Where are you going then?' he asked.

An awkward silence followed during which the thought occurred to me that our objective was actually somewhat vague. We'd come here with the intention of integrating with these people but we hadn't given much thought as to how this would be achieved. Ultimately it was Harcourt who replied.

'Well, there's no hard and fast destination,' he said. 'It's really a question of where we would be most readily absorbed.'

'So you're not going, you're staying.'

'That's the plan, yes.'

Mr Alder furrowed his brow and thought for a moment.

'There's a reception centre further along the coast,' he said, 'but I very much doubt if…'

Before he could finish speaking Harcourt interjected.

'A reception centre!' he exclaimed. 'That sounds like the ideal place!'

I sensed that Mr Alder would have had more to add if he'd been given the chance. Instead, he yielded in the face of Harcourt's enthusiasm. He intoned a few directions, thanked us for the tea and cake and then began walking back towards his hut. I told the others about the impending fine.

'According to the counterfoil,' I said, 'it has to be paid within twenty eight days.'

'Well, that allows us plenty of time to establish some goodwill,' said Harcourt. 'I'm certain they'll find it in themselves to forgive and forget. Meanwhile we need to present ourselves at this reception centre he told us about.'

Everyone concurred except Johnson who to my surprise voiced some reservations.

'I can't help wondering,' he said, 'whether we might have read the situation wrongly.'

'How do you mean?' enquired Harcourt.

'Well, if they've gone to the trouble of setting up a reception centre it suggests that we're not the first to arrive on these shores. We consider ourselves to be pioneers but evidently we've been beaten to it. For all we know there could have been hundreds before us.'

'Now you come to mention it,' said Kingsnorth. 'The map has several points marked with the letters RC. I've been pondering what they might indicate.'

He produced the map and opened it up on the ground. On close examination we discovered multiple RC references scattered along the coastline. They were especially common in the vicinity of harbours and seaside resorts.

If Harcourt was disappointed at this revelation he certainly didn't show it.

'I imagine,' he declared, 'that these reception centres will make our quest even easier. The authorities here are obviously prepared to accept incomers and have made the appropriate arrangements.'

Johnson began to say something and then seemed to change his mind. After that he remained silent as we cleared up and got ready to head along the coast. It was agreed that somebody needed to stay behind to look after the camp and keep an eye on the boat. I thought Harcourt might choose Johnson for this duty but instead he appointed Kingsnorth. We took a bag of provisions with us and set off around midday.

While we'd been engaged in our assorted tasks we'd failed to notice that a small crowd of people had gathered behind the railings on the seafront. They appeared to me as though they were waiting for something. The weather had warmed up nicely during the morning but for no apparent reason the beach was relatively empty. Now, as we climbed the stone stairway, I saw that most members of the crowd were clutching pink tickets in their hands. They moved aside to let us through and we thanked them politely. There was little response. A few managed a nod of acknowledgement but that was all. As we continued along the seafront I happened to glance back. It seemed that the moment we'd gone the crowd of people had started swarming down the stairway and onto the beach. Many of them collected deckchairs from the stack and set them up at various points. Some took off their clothes and went swimming in the sea. Others strolled along the tide line picking up shells. I peered across at our camp and spotted Kingsnorth making some adjustments to one of the tents. None of the beachgoers went anywhere near him.

Further along the seafront we passed a number of shops and a bank. Signs on their doors proclaimed that they were all CLOSED FOR LUNCH.

'Funny way of doing business,' said Harcourt. 'I would have thought this was their busiest time of day.'

'Perhaps they're too prosperous to care,' I suggested.

'So why are they so unhappy?'

'I think it could be a while before we know the answer.'

Mr Alder had instructed us to follow the seafront eastward until it joined the main coast road. We admired a number of carefully-tended flower beds on the way in addition to some sparkling water fountains and a bandstand: more evidence of prosperity (or at least a satisfactory level of well-being). There were flags flying too, though we noticed that the ones on public buildings (an elaborate design in red, white and blue) were markedly different to those on many flats and houses (a simple red and white). Presumably they were both regarded as national flags and we began to wonder whether this might indicate a division of loyalties that we were unaware of. Maybe there existed some kind of hidden rivalry between certain sections of the population. The subsequent sighting of a third kind of flag swiftly dispelled this idea. There was a row of them fluttering high on their poles, all identical, displaying the logo of an internationally popular canned drink. The further we proceeded the greater the variety of flags we encountered (including a flag that was plainly foreign and others that represented assorted football teams) and eventually we concluded that all these different flags were evidence not of mutual intolerance but rather an attempt at gaiety.

'They're purely for decorative purposes,' announced Harcourt, 'intended I suppose to cheer everyone up.'

By now we had reached the coast road where we started seeing the first signposts for the reception centre (distance: 3 miles). The flow of traffic was fairly heavy but we managed to cross over to the landward side during a slight lull. A moment later a van pulled up beside us. It was flying the red and white flag we'd seen on some of the houses. There were two men in navy blue overalls on board. The man in the passenger seat wound down his window.

'Going to the reception centre?' he enquired.

'Yes,' said Harcourt. 'How did you guess?'

'Stands to reason really. Nobody walks along this stretch of road. Not usually anyway.'

'Hop in,' said the driver. 'We'll give you a lift.'

'Very kind of you. Thanks.'

'That's alright,' came the reply. 'The sooner we get you there the sooner we get you out.'

His companion alighted from the van and opened a sliding door. The interior was stacked with an assortment of tools but we all managed to squeeze in. He slid the door shut and returned to his place in the passenger seat.

'Everybody sitting comfortably?' asked the driver over his shoulder.

'Yes, thanks.'

'Okay, next stop the reception centre.'

The two men kept grinning at one another as we sped off down the road. I couldn't quite see what was so amusing but they were good-natured enough. Evidently they weren't the dejected souls we'd been told about. On the contrary, it all seemed like a game to them, a bit of a laugh, which I thought was an encouraging sign.

The driver introduced himself as Andy.

'We're both called Andy,' said his passenger. This was another cause of joviality between them.

Harcourt reciprocated by introducing the three of us by name.

'Where are you chaps from then?' said Andy the first.

Harcourt told him and the two of them exchanged glances.

'We don't get many people from there,' said the second Andy. 'What are you supposed to be running away from? Starvation? Warfare? Slavery? Disease? Don't tell me, I'll guess: poverty?'

'None of those actually,' said Harcourt. 'As a matter of fact we're not running away from anything. We've come to help you.'

Yet more merriment.

'Oh yes? How are you going to do that then?'

'By working in your midst.'

'You mean taking our jobs?'

'If it helps, yes.'

'Ha ha ha!'

At this point Andy the second managed to suppress his mirth and turned around in his seat to address us all.

'Look, chaps,' he said. 'Nothing personal but if you tell them that story at the reception centre they'll laugh you straight out of court. It's best to be honest and let them know the real reason you're here. Otherwise you might as well get back in your boat and go home now.'

'That would save a lot of time and money,' murmured the other Andy.

'Thanks for the advice,' said Harcourt, 'but actually we're quite determined to see our mission through. We've all invested rather a lot of personal capital in this endeavour.'

'Suit yourself.'

The pair of them were plainly impressed by Harcourt's declaration of intent. They made no further comment and became markedly silent during the latter part of the journey.

From where I was sitting I could just about see through a segment of the windscreen and I now noticed that there was a high chainlink fence on our right hand side. Beyond the fence were a number of prefabricated cabins built on a piece of land that jutted into the sea. Ahead of us was a gate with a large sign:

NATIONAL RECEPTION AND PROCESSING CENTRE

The gate was closed. Outside it stood a group of men holding placards. Our van pulled up in a lay-by at the opposite side of the road.

'Hello,' said Andy the driver. 'What's going on here?'

He wound down his window and called across to the men.

'Morning, chaps! We've got some customers for you!'

Now that we'd stopped I could only see the road in front of us and occasional vehicles passing by. A muffled voice from somewhere near the gate replied to Andy.

'Sorry,' it said. 'Processing is suspended.'
'What? Are you on strike or something?'
'Yes.'
'Why?'
'Pay and conditions.'
'Till when?'
'It's indefinite.'

'So you can't take these people?'
'Which people?'
'In our van.'
'No, sorry.'
'For fuck's sake,' snapped the other Andy. 'Greedy fuckers. All they do is fill in a few forms.'
'Not proper work, is it?' uttered his mate. 'Dealing with a boatload of...' He broke off before turning to speak to the three of us.
'Well, nobody can say we haven't tried,' he said, 'but we've got some malingerers in this country who don't want to work. Apparently they're on strike.'
'What shall we do then?' said Harcourt.
'We'll have to drop you here.'
Andy the second got out and slid open the side door.
'Like I told you,' he said. 'Nothing personal.'
We'd just begun stepping out onto the pavement when some of the men from the gate came striding across the road. They appeared rather concerned. One of them spoke to Andy.
'You can't leave them here,' he said.
'Why not?'
'It's illegal to traffic people.'

'We're not trafficking. We're just trying to help them.'

'Well, I'm afraid you'll have to keep them with you until the centre reopens.'

'But you've just told us you're on indefinite strike!'

The man shrugged his shoulders.

'Sorry,' he said, 'but that's the way it is.'

By this time we'd been joined by the other Andy.

'If you're supposed to be on strike,' he said, 'how come you're here giving us orders?'

'I'm just advising you of the situation.'

This made Andy bristle a little. He jabbed a finger.

'Well, I'm advising you,' he said, 'that we're leaving them here and you can't do a thing about it. You're on strike, don't forget.'

'Yes, we are,' agreed the man, 'but do you see that mast over the road there?'

Andy glanced at the mast.

'Yes, what about it?'

'It's got cameras on it recording the registration numbers of all vehicles depositing transients outside the gate.'

'For fuck's sake!' said Andy.

He stepped aside to consult with the other Andy. Meanwhile the men from the gate stood silently regarding us all.

'Can I make a suggestion?' offered Harcourt. 'Why don't my companions and I simply make our way on foot back to the beach?'

'Can't do that,' said the Andy the driver. 'These cunts will get it on camera and blame us.'

Evidently the men overheard his comment.

'We're not cunts,' said one of them. 'It's just our job.'

'But you're not doing it.'

'That's because we're standing up for better pay and conditions.'

'Don't give me that,' said Andy, turning to face him. 'You're lucky you've got a job. You're not even from around here.'

'No, we're not! Nobody around here would do the job we have to do!'

'That's your problem, mate! Why don't you go back up north where you came from if you don't like it?'

'Don't worry, we intend to!'

'The sooner the better!'

The other Andy now intervened and led his partner aside.

'Leave it, Kev,' he murmured. 'They're not worth it. Come on. Let's go.'

'Well, what are we going to do with this lot?'

'They'll have to come with us for the time being.'

'But then we'll be stuck with them.'

'We'll think of something.'

Next moment they were ordering us into the van before climbing into their own seats and slamming the doors.

'Cunts,' said the second Andy as he drove us all away.

3

There was a long silence until eventually Harcourt decided to break the ice.

'Sorry about all that,' he said. 'Our fault I'm afraid. We didn't realise we'd run into such a sensitive state of affairs.'

'Forget about it,' came the reply from the driving seat.

'Actually we're a bit confused about your names. Did you say you were both called Andy?'

'Yes, we did, but we were only joking. My name's Kevin.'

'And mine's Pete.'

'Oh, right.'

'What were yours again?'

Harcourt repeated the introductions.

'Okay, got them this time.'

There was another long silence and then Pete said something quietly to Kevin. There then followed a murmured conversation between them. Eventually they reached some kind of agreement and Pete turned to us.

'Do you chaps mind getting your hands dirty?' he enquired.

'No, not at all,' replied Harcourt.

'It's just that we've got this contract we're a bit behind on. It involves cleaning machinery in a factory. Would you mind helping us get it finished?'

Harcourt looked questioningly at Johnson and me. We both nodded.

'Yes, that fine.'

'We'll pay you a few quid, of course, and you can sleep there until you get sorted out.'

The two of them fell silent again.

I turned to Harcourt.

'What about Kingsnorth?' I asked.

'He should be alright,' he said. 'He's got plenty of supplies.'

'Ah, yes.'

The van continued along the coast road for several miles before making a left turn towards an industrial estate. We made a few more turns until finally reversing into an enclosed yard. Pete got out and opened the sliding door.

'Right, you're not really supposed to be here so when I give you the signal get as quick as you can to that unit over there.'

Kevin, meanwhile, had gone across to a roller door, inserted a key and pressed a button. He waited for seven or eight seconds as the door rose slowly upwards and then he gave Pete a nod.

'Okay, off you go.'

The three of us leapt from the van and sprinted across the yard. Pete followed us casually carrying our bag of provisions. Once we were all inside the unit Kevin lowered the roller doors again and switched on some strip lights. There was a bare concrete floor and the place was cold and sunless. As far as we could see there were large machines standing in rows. I wasn't sure what they were for but they looked important. Pete and Kevin then showed us into a side room where there was a sink and draining board, a worktop with an electric kettle and several wooden chairs. In the corner was a sofa that had plainly seen better days. It was finished in brown imitation leather. There was also a plastic dustbin full of long-handled brushes.

'Alright,' said Pete. 'If you all get a brush each I'll show you what needs doing.'

He led us across to the first machine.

'It doesn't look too bad on the outside,' he said, 'but inside it's filthy. There's a build-up of soot you see and it's all got to be cleaned out. They've been waiting weeks for us to get it done but we've fallen a bit behind. Be really helpful if you could get it moved on a bit.'

He indicated an opening at the side of the machine.

'What you've got to do,' he continued, 'is crawl under there and brush it all out. Who wants to give it a try first?'

Johnson stepped forward with his brush and we watched as he began work.

'That's the way,' said Pete. 'Then you shovel it all into those bins over there.'

Once they were certain we knew what we had to do, Kevin and Pete informed us that they would leave us to it.

'You can use the kitchen when you want,' said Kevin. 'You've got a kettle and there should be some tea underneath the sink. No milk I'm afraid but I expect you'll manage. Make sure you turn all the lights off at bedtime and if anybody asks why you're here tell them you're the live-in caretakers. Got that?'

'So you're going off, are you?' enquired Harcourt.

'Yes,' replied Kevin. 'We need to go and finish another job but we'll be back in the morning.'

With that they left, closing the roller door behind them so that we were effectively trapped inside.

'Not quite what we had in mind,' remarked Harcourt, 'but at least we're getting to know some of them.'

'So you don't think they're exploiting us?' said Johnson.

'I shouldn't think so. They hardly seem the type to do that kind of thing and don't forget they mentioned about paying us.'

'It would be helpful to have some money,' I pointed out. 'Especially as we've got that fine to pay.'

After a light snack we set about our task. The three of us toiled for hour after hour cleaning those machines and clearing away the soot. When the bins were full we went and found some more in the depths of the factory. We'd agreed that the only place we could possibly sleep was on the sofa and there was only room for one at a time. Therefore we decided to work through the night taking turns to have a break. Needless to say it was filthy work. We were covered in soot from the moment we started and we had to be careful not to get it in our eyes. It brushed off easily enough, however, so we accepted the fact that we might appear a little grubby and simply got on with it. I was last to take a turn on the sofa. I flopped down just before dawn, fell asleep straightaway and was woken a couple of hours later by the sound of the roller door opening.

'Who left all the lights on?' demanded an irate voice.

A few seconds later Kevin marched into the kitchen and threw a master switch. Immediately all the strip lights went out. I swung my legs off the sofa and stood up, still feeling rather sleepy.

'We told you to turn them off at bedtime,' Kevin barked. 'Where are the other two?'

'They're still inside the factory,' I said. 'We worked overnight.'

A look of surprise crossed his face.

'What? The whole night?'

'Yes.'

At that moment we were joined by Pete. He was carrying a small stack of navy blue overalls.

'We're lucky the security guys didn't come snooping around,' Kevin told him. 'These plonkers left all the lights on.'

There were footsteps outside the kitchen. It was Harcourt and Johnson. They were both covered with a layer of soot.

'We can't see what we're doing with the lights out,' said Harcourt. 'Fortunately we've finished. We were just sweeping up.'

Kevin and Pete glanced at one another and then without another word went out to inspect the machinery by torchlight. When they came back their mood had changed entirely. We were going through our provisions pondering what to have for breakfast when they returned with big smiles on their faces.

'Excellent job,' said Kevin. 'Very tidy too. Not a trace of soot on the factory floor.'

Pete offered us the navy blue overalls.

'You can have these if you like. Sorry we didn't provide them before but better late than never.'

He showed us into a washroom where we could change and get cleaned up. After some deliberation we decided to wear the overalls directly over our vests and underpants. We put our dirty shirts and trousers in an empty bin liner.

'Give me those and I'll get them laundered for you sometime,' said Pete. 'It's the least we can do.'

The two of them plainly had some further plan in mind because they then offered to take us for breakfast. They told us to grab our stuff and get ourselves across to the van 'fairly smartish'. Once we were inside we had to wait almost half an hour during which time they attended to some other business at the far end of the factory. Johnson remarked that matters seemed to be moving beyond our control. He proposed making a break from Kevin and Pete while we still had the chance.

'We could just walk away now,' he suggested.

'Well, I'm not turning down breakfast,' I said. 'I'm starving and, besides, we don't really know where we are.'

Harcourt agreed with me.

'I think we should stick to our present course for the moment,' he said.

With conspicuous reluctance Johnson deferred to Harcourt's judgement. We then continued waiting for Pete and Kevin and eventually they returned. Pete was carrying the bin liner that contained our dirty clothes. He tossed it onto the pile of tools.

'Right,' he said, closing the sliding door. 'Breakfast.'

We drove another few miles, the van making numerous twists and turns so that we became completely disorientated, and finally we pulled up outside a cafe. There were several other vans parked nearby (all flying red and white flags).

'I'll go and have a word,' said Pete.

He walked over to the cafe, opened the door and spoke to somebody inside. A minute later he came back.

'Follow me,' he said, and we all clambered out of the van.

The cafe was about half full. Pete directed Harcourt, Johnson and me to sit at a corner table away from the window. He and Kevin sat in the opposite corner and talked to the occupants of a neighbouring table whom they clearly knew. Kevin passed some comment and they all laughed. Generally, however, the level of conversation in the cafe was quite subdued.

Almost every customer sat reading the same newspaper and had little to say. After a while a waitress came over to our table with a tray and we received a plate of eggs, chips and beans apiece as well as bread and butter and a mug of tea. We all thanked her politely but she said nothing in reply. When he heard our voices Pete looked across at us and put a finger to his lips. This was the first time since we'd entered the cafe that either he or Kevin had acknowledged our presence: mostly they just ignored us. We complied with his instruction and remained silent for the rest of our visit. A sign above the till indicated that second teas were free with all breakfasts and in due course these arrived. I gave the waitress a smile and she smiled in return.

After about half an hour Pete and Kevin's acquaintances from the neighbouring table folded their newspapers and rose to leave. They thanked the staff behind the counter profusely, said goodbye to Pete and Kevin even more profusely and then gave our table a wink as they departed. Again it struck me that these people were much less downcast than we'd been led to believe. Next minute Pete signalled that it was time to go. He herded us out of the place while

Kevin went to the counter to pay for the breakfasts. The occupants of several other tables glanced in our direction as we headed for the door before returning to peruse their newspapers.

Once we were all back in the van Kevin turned around in the driving seat to speak to us.

'Breakfast alright?' he began.

'Yes, thank you,' said Harcourt. 'Very nice.'

'Good.'

'We've been going there for years,' added Pete.

'Listen, chaps,' Kevin continued. 'You did a good job with that cleaning and we'd like to offer you some more work on the same basis.'

Harcourt nodded but gave no immediate reply.

'Problem is,' said Kevin, 'we have to keep it a bit quiet because you're probably not registered for tax or national insurance are you?'

'No,' I said.

'Then there's the question of accommodation. Where are you staying at present?'

'We've built a camp on the beach near where you picked us up.'

'What? Tents?'

'Yes.'

'Blimey,' said Pete. 'That's hardly going to make you very popular with the locals.'

'They've been alright so far.'

'Believe me, they won't put up with it for long.'

The two of them conferred for a moment or two before Kevin resumed.

'Would you be prepared to stay in your tents if we moved them somewhere else?'

'Suppose so,' I said. 'Yes.'

'It's just that there's this fairground we know about,' Kevin went on. 'They only use it once a year and the rest of the time it stands empty. You could put your tents up and nobody would be any the wiser.'

'So we're going to be exhibits at a fairground, are we?' said Johnson, finally ending his silence.

'No,' said Pete. 'You don't understand. You'd be hidden from view.'

'I understand perfectly well,' Johnson replied, 'and I can see right through your little game.'

'If you don't like it, mate,' snapped Kevin, 'you can go now!'

'Yes, I think I will.'

Harcourt looked alarmed.

'Surely you're not just going to rush off?'

'Watch me,' said Johnson.

He grabbed the inside handle of the sliding door but it wouldn't open.

'Hang on,' said Pete. 'It's locked.'

'Why is it locked?' Johnson demanded. 'Are you trying to keep us prisoner or something?'

He started banging on the door.

'Steady, Johnson,' I said.

'It locks itself when the key's in the ignition,' said Kevin. 'Calm down a sec and Pete'll let you out.'

Pete duly obliged and next moment the door slid open. Johnson scrambled out and began stalking away down the road.

'Johnson!' I shouted but he ignored me.

'I should let him go if I were you,' said Pete. 'He's the sort who gives you lot a bad reputation.'

'Actually he's a very hard worker,' said Harcourt. 'He was the first to step forward at the factory.'

'Maybe so,' said Pete, 'but we can't have people mouthing off like that. He's got to remember he's a guest in this country.'

'Anyone else want to leave?' said Kevin.

'No,' I said.

'No,' said Harcourt.

'Right.'

Pete slammed the door shut and got back in the van. I looked across at Harcourt.

'Johnson should be alright,' I murmured. 'He's very resourceful.'

Harcourt shrugged but gave no answer.

'Right,' said Kevin, starting the engine. 'Let's go and get these tents.'

The route he took was circuitous because, as he explained, he wanted to go nowhere near the reception centre. We eventually rejoined the coast road much further west and pulled into a lay-by. During the journey Pete and Kevin had formulated the details of the plan.

'You'll have to walk from this point,' said Pete. 'Go down that hill and you'll come out at the far end of the beach. Take your tents down and stay with them until it's dark. We'll meet you back here at ten o'clock tonight. Alright?'

'Alright,' I replied.

I noticed that Harcourt was beginning to take very much a back seat when it came to the arrangements. A lot of his earlier enthusiasm seemed to be wearing off as the reality of our situation gradually dawned on him. In consequence it was me who did most of the liaising with Kevin and Pete. They bibbed their horn as they drove away and the two of us set off down the hill. We were still wearing our navy blue overalls and nobody we passed paid us the slightest attention. At the far end of the beach we descended a stone stairway and headed for our encampment. It was now early afternoon. A breeze had got up and the tide was coming in. At last we spotted our boat. It was lying at a peculiar angle with seawater lapping around it.

'Why isn't it floating?' I said, quickening my pace.

The previous day we'd made sure the boat was properly secured and it should have simply risen up with the tide. Instead, however, it had sunk. Further up the beach we saw Kingsnorth sitting on a stack of folded tents looking most disconsolate. We marched up to him and demanded an explanation.

'Why didn't you drag the boat out of the water?' I asked.

'I tried,' he said, 'but I couldn't move it on my own and nobody around here offered any help.'

He went on to tell us that there'd been a raid during the night. While he was asleep a group of people had come and drilled holes in the boat. They'd also let all the tents down. Being on his own he'd been unable to stop them. He'd realised that they were bound to come back and do it again if they had the chance so he'd decided to fold the tents away and await our return.

'What could they hope to achieve by drilling holes in the boat?' said Harcourt.

'Maybe they want us to leave,' said Kingsnorth.

'Well, we can hardly leave if the boat won't float!'

'They probably didn't think of that.'

Fortunately Kingsnorth had managed to save our provisions. We had some lunch and told him about the proposed move to another location. He agreed it was our most favourable option.

'Not much fun to be had on this beach,' he said. 'Everybody's been giving me the cold shoulder.'

'I suppose we'll have to abandon the boat,' said Harcourt.

'Yes, for the time being,' I replied, 'but we might be able to recover it at a later date.'

We settled down and waited for darkness to fall.

4

Pete and Kevin turned up late for the rendezvous. My companions and I arrived punctually at ten o'clock carrying the tents and all our provisions but they were nowhere to be seen. Both Harcourt and Kingsnorth immediately expressed their doubts so I doubled my efforts to reassure them.

'We'll just have to be patient,' I said. 'Don't forget it's in their interests not to let us down.'

Eventually, at around ten forty-five, we saw a flash of headlights and the van pulled into the lay-by.

'Sorry for the wait,' said Pete. 'We stopped at the pub for a swift half but it transformed into a couple of pints.'

We introduced Kingsnorth and then got our stuff on board. Straightaway I noticed that our bag of clothes was still lying where Pete had left it. I realised it was probably premature to remind him about getting them laundered just yet. Instead, I concentrated on trying to keep track of the route we took on our journey. I thought it important to know exactly where we were being taken. For reasons of their own Pete and Kevin had been rather vague about the precise whereabouts of the fairground so I decided to make a mental note of all the left and right turns we made. I also tried to memorise the names shown on road signs. I soon gathered that we were travelling inland and I reckoned we'd gone about five miles when the van passed under a railway arch. It slowed down and stopped in a lay-by. Pete wound down his window and peered into the gloom.

'Entrance should be along here somewhere,' he said. 'Ah, yes, there it is.'

He got out of the van and walked across to where a galvanised chain had been slung between two wooden posts about fifteen feet apart. He unfastened the chain and moved it to one side. Kevin then manoeuvred the van between the posts and onto a concrete road. This was partially overgrown with weeds and bushes. Pete rejoined us and we proceeded cautiously along the road guided only by the headlights. After a couple of hundred yards the concrete petered out and we came to a halt. Ahead of us lay an area of rough grass. It's full extent was indistinct because it was lost in shadows but there was clearly enough room to pitch our tents.

'This do you?' said Kevin.

'Yes,' I said. 'Looks fine.'

'Any water?' Kingsnorth enquired.

'Should be a standpipe over there.'

He gestured into the darkness.

After that it was a simple matter of unloading our gear and setting up camp. Initially we worked in the van's headlights but then the moon came out and Kevin declared that it was plenty bright enough to see by. He was plainly anxious to get away as quickly as possible. Next moment he and Pete were saying goodnight with a promise to be in touch very soon. We watched as the van performed a three point turn and trundled back up the concrete road. When its taillights disappeared it occurred to me that we'd staked our whole future on Kevin and Pete. Stuck in this hidden corner we were now obliged to wait until they came back. I was about to discuss the situation with Harcourt and Kingsnorth when a loud roaring noise announced the passing of a train quite nearby and above us. Thirty seconds later it was gone but then another train went past a little further away. In the moonlight we carried out a brief investigation and established that we were hemmed in between two railway embankments.

'Odd place for a fairground,' remarked Harcourt.

'Well, Kevin mentioned that they only use it once a year,' I said. 'They probably get it rent-free. This piece of land can't be much use for anything else.'

'Handy for us though.'

'As a temporary base, yes.'

Harcourt and I were quite tired from the previous night's exertions and we were soon talking about bedding down. Before retiring, however, Harcourt decided to walk up to the main road to make certain the galvanised chain had been put back in place.

'No point in taking chances,' he remarked. 'We don't really want to attract too much attention to ourselves.'

I went with him and we'd soon verified that, yes, the chain was indeed in place. The only difference was that it was now secured with a padlock.

'I'm sure the padlock wasn't there when we came in,' said Harcourt. 'Perhaps Kevin and Pete are trying to deter unwanted visitors.'

'Yes, perhaps,' I said, 'though to my mind it seems a rather unnecessary precaution.'

Not until the following morning were we able to get a proper look at our new home. We were woken at dawn by the sound of a train going by. When we emerged from our tents we saw that we were in a narrow triangle of land where two railway embankments converged into one. Moss-covered post and wire fences ran along the foot of the embankments which were both engulfed with brambles. At the apex of the triangle stood a huge electricity pylon that emitted a dull humming noise. Nearby was a stack of wooden pallets. In another corner were the remains of a brick hut without a roof. Beside it was the standpipe Kevin had mentioned. The concrete road led through thick undergrowth to the main road where we could hear the rumble of distant traffic. Meanwhile passenger and goods trains continued to go past at regular intervals.

A tattered notice informed us that Barry Barton's Funfair had been here about three months ago. Judging by the size of the piece of ground it can't have been a very large enterprise: there was just enough space for some dodgems, a roundabout, a helter-skelter and four or five stalls. Nevertheless the place must have been noisy when it was in full swing and the generators were all working (not to mention the passing trains).

'They've done their best to make it jolly,' said Harcourt.

He indicated some faded bunting that was strung on poles between the brick hut and the pylon.

'It doesn't look as though anybody's been here since then,' I said. 'The grass is all long and wavy except where we've flattened it.'

We checked our provisions and confirmed that we had enough to last us for a few more days. I then suggested we went up to the road to try and get a better overall picture of our surroundings. Harcourt said he wasn't sure this was a good idea when we were supposed to be maintaining a low profile.

'Well, we can't just stay here hiding all day long,' I said. 'We're meant to be mixing with these people not skulking around.'

'I'd hardly call it hiding,' said Kingsnorth. 'Not with these trains going by every few minutes.'

He had a point there. The main reason Kevin and Pete had suggested moving us to the fairground was because it couldn't be seen from the road. Evidently they hadn't considered its proximity to the railway lines. As if to corroborate Kingsnorth's observation a passenger train went hurtling past a moment later. The embankment was quite high and it was difficult to tell whether anyone on board would notice us if they happened to be looking out of the window. Even if they did see us they'd have no idea who we were. All the same an element of doubt had arisen and I could see that Harcourt was worried. He then proposed that we should take down our tents during daylight hours. I went along with the plan just to keep him reassured but privately I thought he was being a little too circumspect.

I didn't really want to abandon my idea of going up to the main road for a wander around so I decided to wait for an hour or two. In the meantime I occupied myself examining the brick hut. It looked as if it had something to do with the railway line and I guessed it had been used as a shelter by the men who built the embankments. This must have been a major project at the time of construction: they were probably here for several weeks. The hut had a floor of packed earth. There was a cast iron stove in the corner with a chimney poking up where the roof should have been. I closed the door and discovered that after all these years it still fitted perfectly in its frame. The tiny window, however, was broken. Vaguely I toyed with the idea of carrying out a few repairs and making the place habitable again. Maybe I could even add a proper tiled floor. I made a mental note to keep my eyes open for some suitable material to fix the roof. I'd just begun taking some rough measurements when I was snapped back into reality by the loud hooting of a horn. I glanced through the window and saw Kevin and Pete's van nosing down the concrete road.

When I got outside I saw that Harcourt and Kingsnorth were busy moving the folded tents. We'd already stacked them up near a fence but for some reason they'd decided to shift them again. This must have alarmed Kevin and Pete because the van stopped abruptly and they both leapt out.

'Going so soon?' said Pete. 'I wouldn't hear of it. Why, our little party's just beginning.'

He spoke with a croaky voice when he uttered these words but Harcourt and Kingsnorth showed no reaction. They merely gazed at him with bemused expressions on their faces.

'Never mind,' he said. 'Where are you chaps off to?'

Quickly I strolled over and joined them.

'Nowhere,' I said. 'We took the tents down so the people on the trains wouldn't see us.'

'Ah, good idea,' said Pete. 'Didn't think of that.'

'Settling in alright?' Kevin enquired.

'Yes, fine, thanks.'

He looked around him.

'Not much to do though, is there?'

'No.'

'Hang on a sec.'

Kevin returned to the van and came back a moment later with another set of navy blue overalls. He handed them to Kingsnorth.

'You'll need these,' he said. 'We've got another job for you if you're interested.'

'Did you manage to get our clothes laundered?' I asked.

Kevin turned to Pete.

'Did you get them done yet?'

'Sorry, no,' Pete replied. 'Could be couple of days.'

'Oh, right,' I said.

'All set to go then?'

'Suppose so.'

They offered no details of what the work involved. Instead, they opened the van's sliding door and directed Harcourt and Kingsnorth to clamber into the back. They then invited me to sit in the front seat between the two of them. Why they'd bestowed this honour upon me was unclear but I complied simply because it was more comfortable in the front.

The van was just approaching the main road when a train went by on the bridge overhead.

'We'll have to watch that,' remarked Kevin. 'Don't want too many prying eyes.'

Even during their brief visit they'd taken care to sling the galvanised chain between the two posts. Pete got out to move it aside and after we'd passed through he replaced it again.

'Did you padlock it?' Kevin asked when he rejoined us.

'Yep.'

'Good.'

Kevin looked at me sideways.

'Just keeping it a bit exclusive,' he said. 'Discouraging trespassers if you see what I mean.'

'Yes,' I said. 'We surmised that was the case.'

'Surmised?'

'Yes.'

He raised his eyebrows and reflected a moment before speaking.

'Where did you say you were from again?'

I told him.

'Oh, yes, that's right,' he said. 'I must admit you understand our language very well. You know more words than me.'

'Thank you.'

'It's much better if we all speak the same language, isn't it? said Pete. 'Better for all concerned.'

I nodded but said nothing.

We pulled onto the main road and I saw immediately that we were heading towards the coast. I was quite pleased that I recognised some of the place names from the previous evening. We soon turned off, however, and not long afterwards reached the edge of a large trading estate. This was a different world again. Behind high spiked railings there were numerous factories, warehouses and offices, all of them newly-built. The estate was a hive of activity. Arriving workers all wore identity tags. Every car had a parking permit displayed on its windscreen. Articulated lorries went in and out of gateways that were equipped with security barriers and manned by uniformed guards. Vehicles and their contents were checked. Dockets were signed and exchanged. Kevin and Pete eyed these transactions with conspicuous disdain as we passed by and I sensed that such regulated precincts were not their natural habitat. They seemed much more at ease after we'd gone another couple of miles. Gradually the swish new buildings receded behind us and were replaced by grimy older ones. Kevin started whistling a tune. On our left appeared a vast industrial complex behind a shabby chainlink fence. Stacked high in a muddy yard were countless steel oil drums. Their paintwork was invariably discoloured. Some of them were dented. Some were smothered with thick layers of grease. Others had indications of rust. Beyond them a series of conveyor belts led into a factory with walls made from corrugated iron. This extended some distance before giving way to another set of conveyors belts and a second yard full of gleaming oil drums freshly painted in yellow and red. A sign on the factory gate said STANDARD CONTAINERS (RECYCLING) LTD. We drove straight past the place, continued for another mile and then turned into a long, narrow road. There were yards on either side enclosed by high breezeblock walls topped with barbed wire. One yard was full of used tyres. Another was jammed with scrap vehicles. At last we came to an entrance on the right with two solid black gates. Kevin pulled up beside them.

'Here we are,' he said.

Pete got out of the van and with some difficulty managed to swing open the gates. Inside the yard were hundreds of very decrepit oil drums. Kevin drove through the entrance and Pete closed the gates behind us.

As soon as I stepped out of the vehicle I became aware of an acrid stench in the air. All across the yard were huge puddles of water coated with an oily film. Some distance away a guard dog was barking. Kevin opened the sliding door and my two companions climbed out. Kingsnorth was now wearing his new overalls. He winced when he breathed in and peered at me questioningly. I gave a shrug because I was just as in the dark as he was. Harcourt, meanwhile, looked a little under the weather.

'Right, chaps,' said Kevin. 'You'll be doing us a big favour if you can get this job moving. It's quite simple. We take the caps off these drums and add a treatment to make them a bit cleaner. Do you want to show them how it's done, Pete?'

'Well, can't you show them?' Pete replied.

Kevin threw Pete a sharp glance, then shook his head and gave an exasperated sigh.

'Oh, alright,' he said at length. 'I suppose it is my turn. Where are the gloves?'

After a brief rummage in the van Pete produced a box full of rubber gauntlets. He handed a pair to Kevin who then moved along the row of oil drums inspecting them as he went. It took him a minute or so to choose one he considered suitable. He manhandled it to the middle of the yard and called the three of us over to join him. Pete, I noticed, remained standing where he was.

Kevin put on his rubber gauntlets and tried to unscrew a small cap on the lid of the drum. It wouldn't move.

'Fuck,' he murmured.

'You'll need the key,' said Pete.

He marched over to the van and returned with a metal lever which he handed to Kevin. He then stepped back again. Kevin fitted the lever onto the cap and gave it a couple of turns. There was a sudden pop and the cap flew off and landed in a puddle. Instantly the acrid smell increased threefold. Kevin coughed, removed his gauntlets and covered his mouth and nose with a handkerchief as fumes emerged from the drum. From where I stood I could see the word REJECT stamped on its lid.

Once he'd recovered from his fit of coughing Kevin put his gauntlets back on and turned the drum on its side. We watched as about a gallon of brown liquid gushed out and flowed across the yard towards a drain.

'Be alright when it's empty,' said Kevin. 'The rest of the job's quite easy. Can you get the crystals, Pete?'

In the corner of the yard was a pallet stacked with plastic sacks. Pete went and fetched one of them and handed it to Kevin, who poured the contents into the oil drum. There was a further emission of fumes. Pete moved away again. Next, Kevin connected a hosepipe to a tap and began filling the drum with water. The fumes got even worse and once more he coughed and spluttered. When the drum was completely full he turned the tap off.

'That's it,' he said. 'You leave it for an hour and then tip it out and the job's done. Easy.'

He then announced that he needed to go and sit in the van for a few minutes. Pete, in the meantime, handed Harcourt, Kingsnorth and me a pair of gauntlets each plus the metal lever.

'Oh, you'll need this as well,' he said.

From the back of the van he produced a large tool that looked like a giant tin opener.

'If the cap's stuck fast and won't come off,' he explained, 'you need to remove the entire lid.'

Harcourt appeared far from happy.

'But aren't these drums rejected for a reason?' he asked.

'No, no,' said Pete quickly. 'That's just a technical category. Once they've been cleaned they'll be ready for recycling.'

'Then they'll go to that factory up the road, will they?' I ventured.

'Actually, no,' said Pete. 'They're a bit fussy along there. We've got another outlet we use.'

'But…'

'No more questions!' he snapped. 'You from the department of trade and industry or something? No, only joking! Ha ha ha! Sorry! But really you don't need to worry about that side of it. Really you don't. That's for us to sort out. Don't forget you're being paid for every drum.'

'When?'

'When the job's done.'

By this time Kevin had returned.

'We do a lot of recycling in this country,' he said. 'Excellent for the environment, of course.'

'Of course,' I repeated.

'Just stack the clean drums in the corner and we'll pop back in an hour or two to see how you're getting on.'

'So you're leaving us again, are you?'

'Yes,' he said. 'Got some other business to see to.'

'Oh, right.'

Kevin gave me a nod.

'You can be in charge.'

He went and spoke quietly to Pete, who then came over to us with an enquiry.

'Do you like fish and chips?'

'Don't know,' I said. 'Never tried them.'

'Ooh, you're in for a treat,' he said. 'We'll bring you some for lunch.'

5

'Lunch' turned out to be quite late in the afternoon. After Kevin and Pete had left us (closing the gates behind them) we had a look around the yard. There was a small office in the far corner which turned out to be locked. We examined the drums one by one and discovered that without exception they were stamped with the word REJECT. Some had additional symbols such as a skull and cross bones, a bright red flame or a large exclamation mark. Plainly they all contained hazardous materials of one kind or another. The drum Kevin had chosen with such care was comparatively less risky but even that disgorged noxious fumes. The sacks of caustic soda crystals bore similar warnings. It seemed we'd landed ourselves a very unpleasant assignment.

I made an attempt to be positive.

'I think if we're very careful we should be alright,' I said. 'Probably need to tie our handkerchiefs over our mouths and noses.'

'All rather questionable if you ask me,' said Kingsnorth. 'I wonder if they've locked the gates from outside?'

He went over to test them and confirmed that, yes, they had locked the gates. We heard a groan and looked across at Harcourt. He was now sitting on the pile of plastic sacks with his head in his hands.

'Are you alright?' I asked.

'No,' he replied. 'I felt rather queasy when I woke up this morning and it's getting slowly worse.'

'This stench can't be helping matters,' remarked Kingsnorth.

'No,' said Harcourt. 'I assure you it isn't.'

'You just stay there for the time being,' I said. 'Us two can make a start and we'll see how it goes.'

We were fairly lucky with the first drum we tried. The cap came off easily and the liquid that poured out appeared harmless enough. We soon had it bubbling away with a mixture of water and caustic soda inside. The second and third drums were equally unchallenging and we began to think we had the job under control.

When we tried to remove the cap from the fourth drum, however, it simply would not budge, even with both of us heaving on the lever. We concluded that we would have to use the giant tin opener and extract the lid completely. It took Kingsnorth a few attempts to master the correct technique but eventually he got the hang of it. Finally he lifted the lid clear and threw it aside. We both peered into the drum. It was a third full of some murky fluid that had set solid.

'Now what do we do?' said Kingsnorth.

'Well, I suppose we just add the mixture and see what happens.'

Five minutes later we stood watching helplessly as the drum exuded a huge cloud of yellowish vapour. Harcourt retreated even further into his corner while Kingsnorth and I pressed our handkerchiefs to our mouths. We had to wait about a quarter of an hour before we could go anywhere near the drum. Just after we'd resumed work I started to feel a little light-headed. Kingsnorth had fallen silent but we pressed on and by midday we had quite a few drums ready. As instructed we left each one for an hour and then tipped out the contents. Very soon the yard was flowing with a combination of chemicals and water. The drain, I noticed, could barely cope with such a quantity. In the meantime our stack of completed drums grew larger and larger. By now we'd learnt to specialise. I took the caps off all the 'easy' drums while Kingsnorth concentrated on removing the lids from the difficult ones. This speeded up the process considerably. My light-headedness hadn't gone away, though, and I suddenly realised it was hours since we'd eaten. I struggled on but I was beginning to flag when at last the gates swung open and Kevin and Pete returned.

They got out of the van and gazed across the yard at Harcourt who was now lying recumbent on the pile of sacks.

'What's the matter with him?' Pete enquired.

'I'm afraid he's not too well,' I said.

'Yah,' said Kevin. 'He'll be alright when he's had his fish and chips.'

It soon transpired that both Harcourt and Kingsnorth had lost their appetites entirely. Neither could face the meal they were being offered. I was famished but even I hesitated when first confronted with a package wrapped in newspaper. Once I'd opened it, however, I was swiftly converted to the allure of fish and chips.

'We took the liberty of adding salt and vinegar,' said Pete.

I also received a fizzy drink in a can. Kingsnorth then announced that I could have his fish and chips if I wanted. I thanked him and accepted them with good grace. Harcourt asked to be excused and climbed stiffly into the back of the van. Kingsnorth followed him.

'It looks as if you've got quite a lot done,' said Kevin. 'Fancy another turn tomorrow?'

'Alright,' I said, 'but we could really do with some protective masks. You know: because of the fumes.'

'We don't normally bother with those,' he said, 'but I expect we can get you some if you insist.'

'And what about our wages?'

'Well, they usually come at the end of the week.'

'It's just that we haven't got any money to buy provisions.'

'What do you want provisions for? We've only just fed you!'

Kevin appeared to be losing patience. He was still holding the third package of fish and chips which he now pressed into my hands.

'Here,' he snapped. 'You might as well have these too.'

Just then Pete interposed.

'Why don't we write them a cheque?' he suggested. 'You know: from the other account.'

As he spoke these words he gave Kevin a meaningful look which I was unable to interpret. Kevin thought for a moment or two before answering.

'Okay then, yes,' he said, 'we'll do that.'

'Can't it be cash?' I asked.

'Sorry, no, we don't carry any with us.'

'Oh.'

'You never know who's going to jump on you these days,' said Pete.

Kevin went over to the van and scrabbled in the glove compartment, eventually returning with a cheque book. There were only a few cheques in it. He wrote on one and tore it out. He didn't bother filling in the stub.

'Right,' he said. 'Here's a cheque to stop you complaining for a while.'

He handed it to me.

'Thanks,' I said. 'What do I do with it?'

'I suppose you're not with a bank?'

'No.'

'Well, in that case you're best bet is a pub.'

'Do pubs cash cheques then?'

'Some do,' he said, 'but be careful or they may try and swindle you.'

I thanked him for his advice and pocketed the cheque.

The pair of them inspected the drums and appeared quite satisfied with what they saw. It was then decided that we'd done enough work for one day and it was time to head for home. When I looked into the van I saw that Harcourt had turned rather pale. He sat motionless on our bag of clothes (still apparently unlaundered) as we all climbed in and prepared to depart. Once again I was in the front seat between Kevin and Pete. When we left the premises they closed the gates but didn't lock them.

'Is that your yard then?' I enquired.

'No,' said Kevin. 'We're doing the job for somebody else.'

He and Pete offered no further explanation about the nature of their dealings and I didn't ask any more questions. Kingsnorth and Harcourt remained silent throughout the journey. As we approached the turn off for the fairground Kevin suddenly decided to drop us directly beneath the railway arch.

'You don't mind walking the last bit do you?'

His tone of voice suggested this was an instruction rather than a request so I felt I had no choice but to oblige. It was still broad daylight so he made us wait until there was no traffic around before urging us to 'leg it' to the top of the concrete road.

'Keep your heads down,' said Pete, as he let us out, 'and we'll pick you up in the morning.'

Unfortunately Harcourt was in no condition to 'leg it'. He staggered along as best he could, helped by Kingsnorth and me, while Kevin and Pete drove away. When we reached the entrance we all bobbed under the galvanised chain and headed down to our sanctuary.

The place was exactly as we'd left it and I had to admit to myself that it was a relief to get home. We erected the tents and I then consumed the third package of fish and chips (Kingsnorth and Harcourt both declined my offer to share them). Afterwards I washed at the standpipe before crawling into my tent and sleeping for a couple of hours. When I awoke it was dark. There was no sign of my companions so I guessed they were still asleep. I decided it was best not to disturb them and instead I set off towards the main road. On our way back from work we'd passed a pub which I thought might offer a chance to cash the cheque. It was at least a mile away but I reasoned that if I walked there and back it would be a useful way to spend the evening. The only problem was that I was still wearing my navy blue overalls and they weren't exactly spotless any more. In consequence I wasn't sure of the reception I would receive. I had no idea whether people in overalls were frowned upon in pubs or if, for example, they were required to use a separate entrance. I realised I still had a lot to learn about the country I thought I'd come to help. Nonetheless I had to start somewhere and the pub seemed as good a place as any.

Needless to say the walk took longer than I expected. Plainly the distance was more than a mile but I used the opportunity to quietly take note of the locality. The main road meandered for a while before joining a tree-lined avenue with houses on either side. Traffic was light and there were few pedestrians apart from me. I passed a playing field and some business premises and then saw ahead of me a parade of shops and a pub called The Wheatsheaf.

I entered a shady porch and was confronted by two inner doors. Behind them I could hear the hum of conversation. The door on the left said: PUBLIC BAR. The door on the right said: SALOON BAR. I chose the public bar on the assumption that it was open to the public. As I went in, however, everybody turned and looked at me. The hum of conversation ceased. It was only a momentary pause and then they all looked away as if they'd been expecting someone else to arrive. Their conversation resumed. Some were sitting at tables. Others stood at the counter. Without exception they had glasses of beer in front of them. I glanced across the room and spotted an empty table in the corner where I immediately went and sat down. Nobody paid me any further attention and I decided that my overalls must be perfectly acceptable. There was a man behind the counter reading a newspaper but he appeared oblivious to my presence. After I'd been sitting there about ten minutes an adjoining door opened and a young woman came in from the saloon bar. I recognised her straightaway as the waitress who'd brought us our eggs, chips and beans in the cafe. She was collecting empty glasses. There were none at my table and she ignored me as she passed by. A few seconds later she returned empty-handed. This time I managed to catch her eye. I smiled at her but she gave no indication of ever having seen me before.

'How do I get served in here?' I enquired.

She pointed at the counter.

'You have to go up to the bar.'

'Oh…I see…thanks.'

I got up and went over.

The man folded his newspaper and peered at me.

'Pint of…?' he asked.

The hum of conversation abated a little.

'I was wondering,' I said, 'if you could cash a cheque.'

The hum ceased altogether. Everyone in the room, it seemed, was now listening. Without a word the man turned and motioned to a sign on the wall behind him:

WE HAVE AN ARRANGEMENT WITH THE BANK:
THEY DON'T SELL BEER
WE DON'T CASH CHEQUES

'Oh, sorry,' I said. 'I didn't realise.'

The silence all around me persisted as I turned and headed for the exit. Next instant, however, I was surprised to hear a howl of laughter.

'Stop!' called the man behind the bar.

I stopped.

'Come back.'

I obeyed his instruction and saw that many of the other customers were grinning at me.

'He's just testing you,' remarked one of them. 'You're obviously a proper worker.'

'Yes, I am,' I said.

While conversation all around returned to its previous level the barman took me aside and examined my cheque. He then confirmed that he was indeed prepared to cash it.

'Of course, we'll have to apply a discount,' he added, 'to cover our risk.'

The discount rate was twenty five percent. I accepted at once and he handed me the appropriate cash.

'So,' he continued, after placing the cheque in his till. 'Pint of?'

At that moment it dawned on me that I needed to spend at least some of my newly-acquired money in the pub, just to show goodwill.

'Beer please,' I said.

'Which?'

He was now standing behind an array of taps with a glass at the ready.

'That one.'

My selection was entirely at random but it earned a nod of approval from several bystanders.

'Good choice,' said the barman as he carefully poured a pint.

I then paid for it and returned to my corner table. During the next hour or two I drank at what I judged to be the same pace as all the other customers. Occasionally I returned to the bar for another pint but I spent most of the time observing (discreetly) the movements of the young woman collecting glasses. To my eyes she looked a little weary as she went about her work, traipsing constantly from table to table, then going behind the counter to load them into a rack. The public bar was getting increasingly busy as the evening passed and she seemed to have a lot to do (from what I could tell she was also attending to the saloon bar). After a while, therefore, I decided to lend a hand. A group of people at a neighbouring table had left several glasses half-full when they departed. They'd also left a jacket draped over the back of a chair. I gathered up the glasses and deposited them on the counter. She appeared quite alarmed when she saw what I'd done and swiftly intervened.

'Those people have only gone outside for a smoke,' she explained. 'They'll be coming back soon.'

'Sorry,' I said. 'Only trying to help.'

'Thanks,' she said with a smile, 'but you needn't have bothered.'

Fortunately the barman (who was also her boss apparently) hadn't noticed the incident because he was occupied serving other drinkers. Swiftly she returned the glasses to their rightful places before resuming her task. I sat down feeling slightly embarrassed about my faux pas. Doubtless she would consider me an interfering fool and do her best to avoid me from now on. I was surprised, then, when half an hour later she suddenly came and sat down beside me. She had a glass of wine in her hand (it looked like a double measure).

'I'm on my break,' she announced, 'so I thought I'd keep you company for a few minutes. You must be rather lonely sitting here on your own.'

'Well, I'm just trying out the pub,' I said. 'I'm new around here.'

'Yes, I thought so.'

'I saw you in the cafe a few days ago.'

'Did you?'

'There were a few of us.'

She peered at me closely and at last showed some recognition.

'Oh yes,' she said, 'you were sitting at the eggs, chips and beans table.'

'Er…yes.'

'We get a lot of people like you coming in.'

'Really?'

'They always sit at the same table.'

'So you still work there do you?'

'Of course.'

'I thought maybe you'd left there to work here.'

'No, I work in both places.'

'So you've got two jobs?'

'Three actually.'

I was astounded. Where I came from people were only allowed one job (and could only work eight hours). No wonder she looked so tired! I offered to buy her another drink but she declined.

'Not when I'm working,' she said. 'Thanks all the same.'

Before she left me I asked what her name was.

'Eva.'

'Are you working tomorrow?'

'Yes, all day.'

6

I don't remember much about the walk back to the fairground. All I know is that I obediently left the pub when 'time at the bar' was declared even though nobody else showed the slightest indication of being ready to depart. There was no sign of Eva so I assumed she was in the saloon bar.

'Night,' said the barman as I went outside.

I'd lost count of how many pints I'd consumed and the fresh air must have quickly taken effect. After that it was mostly a blur. I clomped along under the street lights, concentrating hard on putting one foot in front of the other, and then negotiated a stretch of unlit road until finally I saw the looming shadow of the railway arch. After the long walk I was beginning to sober up. Or so I thought. I wandered around in the dark for several minutes and eventually managed to find the galvanised chain. The padlock was still in place: for a few seconds I tried to recall its significance but soon gave up. I almost stumbled as I bobbed beneath the chain and then set off in pitch blackness down towards the tents. Although I was no great distance from the main road it felt very remote here. All was quiet and at one point I paused for a while to listen. Maybe a train would come past and break the silence. None did, so I concluded that they'd stopped running for the night. Then, as I stood swaying in the gloom, I heard faint voices from somewhere above me on the railway embankment. From the sound of it there were two or three men talking to one another. I also heard a metallic clanking noise which I was unable to identify. The beam of a torch flashed briefly through the air. I continued listening for some minutes but evidently the men were moving away along the line. I waited until I was certain they'd gone and then felt my way to my tent. By now the day's work had caught up with me and no sooner had I crept inside than I was fast asleep.

Next morning I woke just as a train went by. I lay there dozing and waited for a second train on the other embankment. That was the usual pattern but today it seemed to be different. The frequency of trains had reduced considerably and when I finally emerged from my tent I discovered the reason why: only one of the lines was open; the other was closed and had men working on it. I could see them moving around in orange high-visibility jackets. They were busily engaged with their various tasks and scarcely glanced in our direction. Even so they can't have helped noticing the little group of tents. With some disquiet I watched another train going past on the opposite embankment. Inside it I imagined countless noses pressed to the carriage windows and all eyes upon us. The truth was dawning. There was no avoiding the fact that we were now under casual surveillance and I began wondering how long we could remain here at the fairground. I was still lost in thought when I was alerted by a noise behind me.

'Pssst!'

I looked around and saw Kevin peeping out of the brick hut. Presumably he was attempting to keep out of sight. He beckoned me to join him so I walked over to the hut and went inside.

'Why aren't you all ready yet?' he demanded. 'You were supposed to meet us up by the main road.'

'Sorry,' I said, 'but the arrangement was rather vague.'

'Where are the others anyway?'

'Don't know. Wait a moment. I'll go and find out.'

I'd been feeling uneasy about the continuing failure to appear of either of my companions. Now, when I looked into Harcourt's tent, I saw that he was in no condition even to get up let alone go to work. He was in a terrible state. I asked him if he had any idea what might be the matter but he just said he wanted to be left alone. Kingsnorth was no better. He said all the chemicals from the day before had given him a headache which he couldn't shake off. I went and got him a drink of water and then returned to the brick hut where Kevin was waiting.

'I'm afraid it'll just be me today,' I informed him. 'The others are both feeling a bit off colour.'

Kevin was far from sympathetic.

'Well, when will they be fit for work then?'

'Not sure really. Sorry.'

He gave his trademark exasperated sigh.

'Come on then,' he said. 'Let's get back to the van.'

Swiftly he marched out of the hut and up the concrete road with me trailing behind him. We dodged under the galvanised chain (padlock still in place) and headed for the van. Kevin had left it in the lay-by and as we approached I saw that Pete was not on board. I asked Kevin where he was.

'He's got our other van today,' he said. 'He'll catch up with us later.'

When I climbed into the passenger seat I was surprised to see two strangers crouched in the back. They were both wearing navy blue overalls.

'I picked them up near the reception centre,' Kevin explained as we began our journey. 'They're still on strike down there and these two had nowhere to go. Meet Gustav and Wolfgang.'

For a moment I suspected these were 'joke' names that Kevin had applied to the new arrivals. When I introduced myself, however, the two of them confirmed that they were indeed called Gustav and Wolfgang.

'They're going to be joining your team,' said Kevin. 'You'll be in charge if you don't mind.'

'Did you get the face masks?' I enquired.

'Not yet.'

'What about our clothes from the laundry?'

'You're very hard to please, aren't you?' Kevin answered. 'Cash that cheque alright?'

'Yes.'

'Right, well, just be patient then.'

I decided to drop the subject of the laundry for the time being. Meanwhile Gustav and Wolfgang chattered away in the back of the van (Gustav especially so). They were both highly enthusiastic about their prospects in this 'new venture' (as they called it). The way they talked anyone would have thought they'd arrived in some kind of promised land where all their aspirations would be fulfilled. It was also clear that they hadn't come to this country to help cure the population of its gloominess. Rather, they were out for themselves and viewed their meeting with Kevin as a stroke of good fortune. Quietly I predicted they were destined for disappointment.

When we arrived at the yard I saw that most of the contaminated water from the day before had now drained away, though there were still a few puddles scattered around.

Unsurprisingly, Kevin soon announced that he would leave us to it.

'Don't forget the face masks,' I said as he departed.

'No, alright, boss,' he replied.

He closed the gates behind him and I then began explaining the cleaning process to Gustav and Wolfgang. I decided to use one of the completed drums from yesterday to demonstrate what needed to be done. I showed them how to remove the caps and the correct method for operating the giant tin opener. Finally I put a tiny quantity of caustic soda inside the drum and added water.

'Obviously the dirty drums require a full measure,' I said. 'This is for demonstration purposes only.'

Because it was their first day the new recruits got stuck into the work with gusto. I suggested they tied handkerchiefs over their mouths and noses but neither of them bothered so I said nothing more on the matter. In the meantime I exercised my privilege as 'charge hand' and kept well clear of any unfinished drums. Once I was certain the two of them knew what they were doing I went and tried the gates and discovered that Kevin hadn't locked them.

'I'll be back in a while,' I said. 'Just carry on as you are.'

I walked out into the road and closed the gates. There was little traffic. I strolled along looking into various yards as I went by to see what was in them. Most served the same general purpose: they were used for storage, cleaning and repairs of assorted items. Some housed mechanical excavators (all painted a grimy yellow) or flatbed lorries. Others contained mounds of sand and gravel. I passed the yard with the barking guard dog and then saw in the distance a low building with a sign on the pavement out front: FISH AND CHIPS.

During my walk an idea had gradually been forming which now came to fruition. I entered the shop and examined the menu chalked up on a blackboard. I noted that there was a choice between cod and plaice. No other customers were present: neither was there anyone behind the counter. Only after about five minutes did a man appear from a back room.

'Yes sir?' he asked.

'Plaice and chips please. Thrice.'

'You mean three plaice and chips?'

'Yes.'

'We haven't got plaice. Just cod.'

'But it says plaice on the blackboard.'

'It always says that,' he said. 'In case we do have plaice.'

'Oh.'

'Cod alright then?'

'Suppose so, yes.'

'Salt and vinegar?'

'Please.'

'Right you are.'

The order took longer than I expected to complete. Apparently they didn't have fish at the ready as I expected (I'd been led to believe that everything was 'instant' in this country) and in consequence I had to wait about twenty minutes. Still, it didn't matter as there was plenty of time. I paid with the remainder of my cash and pocketed a small amount of change. The money didn't seem to have gone very far but nevertheless I was feeling rather pleased with myself.

When I got back to the yard I saw that Gustav and Wolfgang had processed a fair amount of drums so I told them it was time for a rest. I noticed they were both now wearing handkerchiefs over their mouths and noses.

'Should be some face masks coming soon,' I informed them.

'Excellent,' said Gustav. 'Those fumes are quite overwhelming.'

They were equally delighted when I presented them with their fish and chips.

'Oh, yes, we've heard of these,' said Wolfgang. 'Very nice.'

I realised I'd forgotten to bring any fizzy drink as an accompaniment.

'We'll have to have tap water today,' I said.

Once we'd all eaten it was swiftly back to work. There were now lots of drums waiting to be tipped over and emptied. I took charge of that job while Gustav and Wolfgang continued opening drums and adding the mixture. It was very late in the afternoon when a horn hooted outside the double gates. A few moments later Kevin swung them open before driving the van into the yard. He was followed by Pete in a similar vehicle flying the same red and white flag. They both got out and called me over to join them.

'Do they have cars where you come from?' Kevin asked.

'Of course,' I replied.

'And vans?'

'Yes.'

'So you've got a driving license, have you?'

'Again, yes.'

'Good.'

'We're going to put your name on our insurance policy,' said Pete. 'It'll help keep our premium down and you can use the van to give Gustav and Wolfgang a ride.'

'Where to?'

'They can come to the fairground with you.'

'Have they got their own tents then?'

'Not sure.'

A brief enquiry established that, no, they hadn't got their own tents.

'Can't they share yours?' said Kevin.

I thought this was a bit of an imposition considering I was barely acquainted with my new co-workers. I also needed to be mindful of Harcourt and Kingsnorth. They'd never even met Gustav and Wolfgang and could possibly object to having the newcomers foisted upon them. On the other hand I realised I had the opportunity to seize an advantage. After all I would be doing Kevin and Pete a big favour if I provided accommodation for their workforce. I decided to negotiate.

'Any chance of another cheque?' I said.

Kevin raised his eyebrows.

'Spent it already?'

'I'm afraid so.'

'Oh, well, yes, I suppose that's alright.'

He went to the van and got the cheque book.

'If you pay me for the three of us,' I said, 'I can pass it on to them.'

Kevin and Pete peered at one another before moving aside for a brief discussion. I saw them nod in agreement and then they rejoined me.

'Okay, that's fine by us,' said Kevin.

'Did you get the face masks?'

'No, sorry, forgot.'

'Well, we could really do with them if we're going to carry out this work properly.'

'Alright, alright. We'll definitely get some tomorrow okay?'

'Okay.'

Kevin gave me a cheque and put the cheque book in his pocket. He then handed me the keys to the van.

'Right,' he said. 'See you here bright and early tomorrow morning.'

'So I'm keeping it overnight, am I?'

'You might as well. Don't park it anywhere obvious and be careful with your driving. The insurance is only third party.'

Gustav and Wolfgang hadn't been consulted about the plan but they appeared amenable enough. I allowed them to sit in the front of the van and then started the engine. Unfortunately I stalled as I moved away. Kevin and Pete were watching and they both shook their heads in mock despair.

'Sorry,' I said, through the open window. 'I'm not accustomed to manual gears. They're viewed as a bit old-fashioned where I come from.'

The second attempt was better. I hooted the horn prior to manoeuvring out onto the road and soon we were heading homeward. Instead of heading directly for the fairground, however, there was a call I wanted to make first. Before leaving I'd happened to glance into the back of the van and noticed the bag of unwashed clothes lying there. Kevin and Pete were plainly not going to honour their promise to get them laundered so I had resolved to take the matter into my own hands. A couple of miles along the road I pulled up next to a laundromat that I'd spotted on our outward journey. I instructed Gustav and Wolfgang to wait while I took the clothes inside. The few remaining coins in my pocket turned out to be just enough to get them washed and dried. The process took well over an hour and when I got back to the van my two passengers were fast asleep. I started up and continued to the fairground.

7

Dusk was approaching when I stopped under the railway arch. My intention was to leave the van there while I took Gustav and Wolfgang down to the encampment and then come back and move it to somewhere less obtrusive. The two of them followed me drowsily through the encroaching darkness.

I was quite pleased to find that Harcourt and Kingsnorth were both up and about. I could see them lurking in the shadows as we drew near. No doubt they were being cautious about unexpected visitors so I quickly set their minds at ease.

'Harcourt, Kingsnorth,' I said. 'This is Gustav and Wolfgang.'

Handshakes were exchanged and I enquired if they were feeling any better.

'I think I'm past the worst of it,' said Harcourt.

'Me too,' added Kingsnorth.

I thought it would be wise not to mention the proposed sharing of tents just yet. Instead, I told them about the van and presented Harcourt with his freshly-laundered clothes. His gratitude was beyond measure.

'At last,' said Harcourt, 'I can take off these damned overalls.'

'Shame about Johnson going off like that,' I remarked. 'I wonder how he's managing?'

'I expect he'll be alright,' said Kingsnorth. 'Johnson's a born survivor.'

I asked about the railwaymen we'd seen on the embankment. Apparently they'd been carrying out some maintenance and had now moved further down the line. Throughout the day they'd shown no interest in our camp.

'I think it's the last we've seen of them,' said Harcourt.

The talk then progressed onto the subject of food. It transpired that our supply of provisions was not exactly running low but would clearly need replenishment sometime in the near future. Meanwhile I proposed a meal for our two guests.

'They've been working hard all day,' I said, 'but at present they've got no money to buy food.'

I knew Harcourt well enough to be sure he would heartily support the idea of helping others. He was happy to share our food with Gustav and Wolfgang and the same went for Kingsnorth. I gave them all sufficient time to befriend one another before mentioning anything about sharing our tents. Again Harcourt's generosity won the day and the appropriate arrangements were made: Gustav and Wolfgang in one tent, Harcourt and Kingsnorth in the second tent and me in the third.

'Right then,' I said. 'I'd better go and move the van. Very handy really. There'll be plenty of room for all five of us in the morning.'

'Where do you propose going then?' Harcourt enquired.

'To work.'

'Oh no,' he said. 'I'm not handling any of those drums. They're obviously quite lethal.'

'Nor me,' said Kingsnorth.

It turned out that the pair of them had spent the afternoon debating our situation and come to the conclusion we were achieving nothing by toiling away at the oil drum yard.

'In fact, we're probably adding to the problems this country faces rather than helping alleviate them,' said Harcourt.

'Well, what are you going to do instead?' I asked.

'We're going to go to the reception centre and see what they have to say.'

'But they're on still on strike,' I countered.

'We'll just have to wait until the matter's settled.'

Harcourt and Kingsnorth didn't seem to understand that it was entirely impractical to merely wait and see what happened. For all they knew the strike could continue for months. Furthermore, I'd been in this country long enough to learn that we weren't entirely welcome here despite our best intentions. If they walked into the reception centre on the day it reopened they could simply be asking for trouble. Lastly there was the question of what they would live on in the interim. We'd already agreed that our stock of provisions wouldn't hold out forever. There was possibly enough for another week but after that we'd be struggling.

I sensed, however, that in their present state of mind there was little point in trying to make them see reason. Perhaps after a while they'd come around to my way of thinking.

'Okay,' I said. 'I'll see you later.'

It was now completely dark. I headed up the concrete road and bobbed underneath the galvanised chain. To my consternation I saw that somebody with a torch was examining the van. When I got closer I noticed a moped parked behind it. I couldn't tell for certain but the person with the torch appeared to be wearing a black and yellow uniform.

I drew nearer still.

'Hello,' I said. 'Is there a problem?'

A woman's voice answered.

'You can't park here.'

She swung her torch towards a sign at the roadside: NO STOPPING AT ANY TIME.

'Sorry,' I said. 'I'll move it.'

'Too late,' she replied. 'I've already issued a ticket.'

She stepped forward to hand it to me and I realised it was Eva. It took me a moment to recover from my surprise.

'So this is your third job,' I said at length.

'Yes.'

'So you won't be in the pub tonight?'

'No. Sorry.'

I gazed with dismay at the parking ticket.

'I can put it under the windscreen wipers if you like,' said Eva.

'No, it's alright,' I said. 'When's it got to be paid?'

'You've got twenty eight days.' She pointed along the road towards the lay-by. 'You should have parked there.'

Eva gave me a smile before returning to her moped, starting up and riding away. I put the ticket in my pocket and climbed into the van. I wasn't sure where I was going to leave it overnight. Kevin had specified somewhere not too obvious so actually I had quite a lot of choice. I'd been harbouring the vague idea of calling at the pub to cash my latest cheque before parking the van. It was disappointing to learn that Eva would not be there but I decided to go to the pub anyway. Obviously I couldn't have much to drink because I was driving: it would have to be two pints at the most.

As I entered the public bar of The Wheatsheaf I saw virtually the same crowd as the night before. They all turned and looked at me as I walked in only to resume their conversations a moment later. It struck me that I should have changed out of my overalls and put my own newly-laundered clothes back on. The truth was that I'd been wearing the overalls so long I'd got completely used to them. Still, it was too late now and nobody seemed to notice anyway.

'Pint of your usual?' enquired the barman.

'Yes, please.' In the same instant I realised I hadn't any cash left. 'Sorry. Can I cash a cheque?'

'Of course.'

There was no examination this evening. He simply put the cheque in his till and gave me my money. I wondered if this meant I'd been accepted into their midst. Probably not but at least it was a start.

Once I'd got my pint I sat down at a table and worked out how to divide the money between my companions and me. The process was quite complicated. I'd completed two days at the oil drum yard whereas Kingsnorth had only done one and Harcourt none at all. I then had to make a secondary calculation for Gustav and Wolfgang. It so happened I'd already arrived at a formula for those two: I would receive fifty percent and they'd get twenty five percent each. Going back to the night we'd done the cleaning at the factory I had to include an adjustment for the absent Johnson who'd presumably forfeited his share. We all took a bit of a hit because of the twenty five percent discount on the cheque and I also needed to allow for the money I'd been given on account (and which I'd already spent). Finally, I would have to make an additional deduction from Gustav and Wolfgang to cover the cost of their fish and chips. When I was satisfied I had it all in order I sat back and enjoyed my beer.

There was a different woman collecting glasses this evening. She had multiple earrings on both ears. I smiled at her a couple of times but she ignored me completely. I decided she wasn't nearly as graceful as Eva.

When I returned to the bar for a second pint the barman didn't even ask what I wanted. He simply filled a glass, gave me a nod and accepted payment. By now I'd gathered that his name was Norman. I had to admit I was beginning to like this pub. I liked the subdued lighting, the flock wallpaper and the heavy velvet curtains at the windows. I also liked the simple pleasure of sitting here drinking beer in peace. All the same there was something nagging at me that I couldn't quite put my finger on: some important matter I'd neglected and which had to be dealt with. I'd first noticed the feeling when Eva issued my parking ticket and mentioned that I had twenty eight days to pay. The phrase seemed familiar but I was at a loss to remember why. I sat down at my table deep in thought and then all at once it came to me: I hadn't paid the fine for the deckchairs!

With some relief I realised that I still had plenty of time left. Even so it was disconcerting to think I'd forgotten about the fine completely. I pictured Mr Alder sitting all alone in his hut. He most likely felt thoroughly let down by our abrupt disappearance from the beach. Therefore I made it my mission to return as soon as possible and pay the fine. Fortunately I was now in possession of the requisite funds.

When last orders were called I resisted the temptation to buy a third pint. Instead, I said goodnight and strolled towards the door.

'Goodnight!' chorused several customers.

When I got outside I paused and gazed all around me. I still hadn't decided where to park the van. In my present mood it struck me as pointless to try and hide it when there were so many similar vehicles around. Why not simply leave it where it was outside the pub? It was a bright moonlit night and the stars were out: perfect for a walk home. I could easily come and collect the van in the morning and then I'd be free to have the extra pint I'd denied myself. The decision was made. With a spring in my step I went back inside and ordered another beer.

'Changed your mind?' said Norman.

'Yes.'

'Well, you cut it fine. We close in a few minutes.'

Actually it was almost twenty minutes before I departed. I stood at the end of the bar and watched as the pub emptied in dribs and drabs. The people appeared reluctant to leave. They wandered away in a slow and haphazard procession until eventually there were only one or two stragglers remaining (including me).

'Come on!' yelled Norman. 'Let's be having you!'

He flicked a switch and the subdued lighting turned suddenly brighter as an overhead fluorescent tube burst into life. Now the innate grubbiness of the pub was revealed in all its glory. Norman and his assistant busied themselves collecting glasses, moving chairs and polishing tables. I drained my glass and left. This time nobody wished me goodnight.

Before starting my journey I checked the van to make sure it was locked properly. Then I set off towards the fairground on foot. After about ten minutes I was beginning to regret my rash decision as the walk was already becoming a slog. I had no choice but to press on, however, and in due course I reached the unlit section of road. I was thankful when at last I saw the railway arch looming ahead of me but then I became aware of a harsh searing noise somewhere not far away. I stopped and listened. It was now quite late in the evening and there was no traffic. The noise persisted and then I noticed a faint glow a few yards from the roadside. As I drew near I realised that the glow was actually caused by sparks flying. There was a pick-up truck parked in the lay-by with a caravan attached. Nearby a man was working with an angle grinder. As far as I could tell he was alone so I continued a little further towards him. I now saw that he was attempting to cut the padlock away from the galvanised chain. He was concentrating on his work and had no idea I was there. I watched mesmerised as the sparks flew.

The noise from the angle grinder was fairly loud and I wondered if they could hear it down at the encampment. To my knowledge there were no houses nearby but I couldn't be sure. The man clearly knew what he was doing and I expected the chain to fall away at any moment. For this reason I thought it would be a good idea to retreat into the shadows. I watched as he abruptly pulled the angle grinder clear of the chain and switched it off. In the same instant the chain fell heavily to the ground. He pulled it to one side before returning to the pick-up truck. After putting the angle grinder in the back he climbed in and started the engine. A few seconds later the headlights came on and the truck began moving forward with the caravan in tow. It turned cautiously between the two posts and proceeded down the concrete road.

I stood in the darkness trying to decide what to do. The arrival of the pick-up truck didn't seem a very good omen to me and I was disinclined to follow it down to the encampment. After some thought I concluded that the only alternative was to walk back and sleep in the van overnight. By now I was quite weary but at least I was getting used to the journey. I was beginning to recognise certain landmarks on the way and I soon found myself striding along the tree-lined avenue. Finally the parade of shops came into view and I reached the van. After fumbling with the keys I crawled inside and stretched out on the front seat. Within seconds I was asleep.

Next thing I knew it was broad daylight and somebody was tapping on the windscreen. Blearily I opened my eyes and saw a man peering in at me. He was wearing the same black and yellow uniform as Eva. I wound down the window.

'You ought to be careful, mate,' he said. 'You can't park here after eight thirty.'

'What time is it now then?' I asked.

'Eight twenty eight.'

'Okay, thanks. I'll move it.'

Swiftly I got behind the wheel and went to start the engine but then I couldn't find the keys. I glanced at the man and saw that he was holding them up between his thumb and forefinger.

'You left them in the door,' he said, before handing them over.

'Thanks again.'

He watched as I fired up the engine, lurched away from the kerb and headed down the road. I'd just started looking for somewhere better to park the van when I suddenly remembered Kevin's injunction to be at the oil drum yard bright and early in the morning. A chill swept through me as I realised that eight thirty was hardly bright and early! Moreover, I still had to go and collect Gustav and Wolfgang! In panic I set off for the fairground as fast as the speed limit would allow.

When I reached the railway arch I slowed down and pulled into the lay-by. I hoped to find Gustav and Wolfgang waiting at the top of the concrete road but there was no sign of them. The galvanised chain was still lying to one side so I decided to save some time by driving down to the encampment. As I approached I saw the caravan parked beside the brick hut. Gustav and Wolfgang were loitering nearby. When they saw me arriving they came over to meet me.

'We waited under the bridge for about an hour,' said Gustav, 'but eventually we got fed up.'

'Well, I'm here now,' I said. 'Have you had any breakfast?'

'No,' he replied. 'Your friends took the provisions with them when they departed.'

I then noticed that two of the tents had vanished. I went and looked inside mine, expecting to find my share of the provisions, but there was nothing.

'They told us they thought you must have abandoned them,' said Wolfgang.

'Because I didn't come back last night?'

'Yes.'

'Did they say where they were going?'

'To the reception centre.'

I asked Gustav and Wolfgang if they'd seen the pick-up truck. They said they'd only heard a vehicle arriving late and leaving very early.

'Right, well, no doubt we'll find out about it later,' I said. 'Meanwhile, we'd better get off to work.'

Soon the three of us were in the van and heading back up the concrete road. I was a bit concerned about being so late and wondered what Kevin and Pete would have to say on the subject. Some acerbic comment no doubt. The fact that I'd had no breakfast made matters worse but I pressed on and hoped for the best. When eventually we arrived at the yard we found the gates closed but not locked. Inside was a huge new consignment of drums all marked REJECT. The completed drums from the day before were nowhere to be seen. Evidently Kevin and Pete had been and gone but it turned out they'd left a note on top of the pile of plastic sacks. It read:

MORNING SLEEPY HEADS.
TRY AND GET THESE DRUMS DONE TODAY
AND WE'LL SEE YOU LATER.

They hadn't bothered signing the note but it was obviously from them. Beside it, to my surprise, was a brand new package containing several face masks. Despite the request to 'try and get the drums done today' the note didn't have a particularly urgent tone. Therefore I decided that before we commenced work we should all go and have some breakfast. I put the face masks safely in the van and we set off towards the cafe. It was a few days since Kevin and Pete had taken us there but I'd been keeping my eyes open during my travels and I now had a pretty good idea where it was. I only made one wrong turning on the way there and presently we pulled up outside. There were a number of vehicles already parked nearby but thankfully no sign of Kevin and Pete's other van. I didn't really want to bump into the pair of them just yet.

'Right,' I said. 'Follow me and sit where I tell you to.'

I led Gustav and Wolfgang into the cafe and directed them to sit at the table in the corner. The other customers sat reading their newspapers and paid us little attention. After placing an order for three lots of eggs, chips and beans plus bread and butter and a mug of tea apiece I went and joined my new workmates. Gustav, I'd recently come to learn, was rather talkative and when I sat down he was already in full flow.

'They're funny people in this country,' he said. 'They like foreign holidays and foreign cars yet they avowedly dislike foreigners.'

'If you say so,' I remarked.

'The only exceptions are foreign footballers.'

As he spoke I noticed one or two people at neighbouring tables glance briefly towards him.

'They dislike foreign laws because they consider them too intrusive,' he continued loudly, 'but their own laws are almost identical.'

More glances.

Gustav was now getting into his stride.

'Their oddest trait,' he announced, 'is their attitude to work. They complain about foreigners taking their jobs but they're reluctant to do the jobs themselves.'

I was starting to wonder how long this unfounded diatribe might go on for when Eva arrived carrying our breakfasts on a tray. She glared reproachfully at Gustav before uttering a few words in a language I didn't understand. Gustav replied in the same language and immediately fell silent. It was clear that he'd been thoroughly chastised. I noted with relief that the customers at the neighbouring tables had all returned to perusing their newspapers.

Eva barely acknowledged my presence as she dealt with the situation but naturally I felt highly indebted to her. She bustled around with her tray and a little later delivered our second mugs of tea.

'Thanks, Eva,' I said. 'This is Gustav and this is Wolfgang.'

'Hello,' she said coldly to the pair of them.

They both nodded and gave deferential smiles.

I lowered my voice.

'Will you be in the pub tonight?'

'Yes,' she said, 'but don't forget I'll be busy.'

'Okay. Might see you later.'

'Alright.'

It was time to go to work so I ushered Gustav and Wolfgang out of the cafe and then went to the counter to settle up for the breakfasts. While I was doing so the thought occurred to me that I effectively held the purse strings for myself, Harcourt, Kingsnorth, Gustav and Wolfgang (not forgetting Johnson of course.) The realisation gave me an odd feeling of empowerment that I'd never formerly experienced. I was beginning to feel like a completely different person to the newcomer who'd landed on these shores less than a week before.

8

It was mid-morning when we got to the yard and began working on the drums. I allotted Gustav and Wolfgang the same tasks as the previous day with Gustav specialising in operating the giant tin opener. That, I thought, would keep him quiet for a bit. After we'd left the cafe he'd resumed his tirade the moment we'd gained the privacy of the van and by now I'd concluded he was a highly opinionated individual. Well, if he wasn't careful he was going to make himself unpopular.

Interestingly enough, neither he nor Wolfgang had yet mentioned the subject of payment for their work. They'd revealed quite early on that they were chiefly motivated by the prospect of earning money but so far they'd failed to enquire about the details. This suggested they trusted me to treat them fairly. Obviously I would do my best to look after their interests as long as they realised I had wider responsibilities too. It was me, for example, who provided their transport and accommodation, me who'd ensured they were issued with proper face masks and me who had to deal with Kevin and Pete. This last role was the most exacting because it was plain that those two were a wily pair of customers with no real sense of loyalty. If Gustav and Wolfgang understood all this then we would get along just fine.

I'd just finished moving some of the completed drums ready for stacking when I noticed that the double gates had swung open slightly. In the gap a man stood regarding the scene before him. The yard was currently awash with the usual mixture of water and chemicals issuing from drums which had recently been tipped over. Meanwhile, Gustav and Wolfgang were measuring caustic soda crystals into the next batch.

The man continued watching for several minutes. He appeared familiar with the process he was observing and I speculated whether he was the 'outlet' Pete had mentioned a few days ago. He certainly had a proprietorial air about him. His clothes were smart but practical and I imagined he was accustomed to hard work if necessity demanded. Eventually he saw me looking over. He stepped inside the gates and closed them before making his way between the puddles towards me. I was unsure if Gustav and Wolfgang were aware of his presence but if they were they didn't show it. They merely carried on toiling away at the other side of the yard. The man approached me and nodded.

'Morning,' he said.

'Morning.'

'I see you've got a nice little operation underway here.'

'Yes, I suppose we have.'

He peered across at Gustav and Wolfgang.

'They work for you, do they?'

'They work under me, yes.'

'The reason I ask is because I've just taken over the lease for this yard. I'll be getting rid of the oil drums and turning it into a car wash.'

'Ah.'

As I absorbed the news I wondered if Kevin and Pete knew anything about it. I was sure that they wouldn't welcome having to vacate the premises (unless, of course, they'd known all along and hadn't bother to tell me). In any case it seemed that my term in the oil drum recycling business would be coming to an end fairly soon. I viewed this outcome with mixed feelings. It goes without saying that I'd liked having money in my pocket during the past few days but at the same time nobody could say the work was enjoyable. On the contrary: it was a monotonous slog. Furthermore, as Harcourt had pointed out, we were hardly achieving our goal of lifting the host nation out of its malaise. The key to that particular conundrum most probably lay elsewhere and not in a desolate yard on an equally desolate road.

I was still pondering all this when the man suddenly introduced himself.

'Sorry, I should have said before, the name's Ted Gresham.'

We shook hands and he then informed me that the equipment for the car wash was due to be installed within a few days. Obviously he would require some operatives for his new venture and he asked me if I knew any likely candidates.

'Well,' I said, gesturing towards Gustav and Wolfgang, 'those two are very hard working.'

'Yes, I can see that,' agreed Gresham, 'but aren't they under contract to you?'

'Sort of,' I said, 'but I could let you have them if it helps you get started.'

'What percentage would you require?'

I plucked a figure out of the air and to my surprise he agreed at once.

'To tell the truth it'll save me a lot of time and trouble,' he said. 'It's very difficult getting hold of dependable people these days. I could actually do with about half a dozen all told if you've any more on your books.'

'I'll see what I can do.'

We then discussed arrangements and he gave me the date when the car wash was scheduled for opening.

'Better get them to turn up the day before,' he suggested, 'so I can show them the ropes.'

After another handshake he departed, closing the gates behind him. To celebrate this turn of events I strolled over to Gustav and Wolfgang and enquired if they were hungry. Inevitably they were so I then went off and got us all some fish and chips accompanied by a fizzy drink. When I got back they were still hard at work. I signalled a break and we all went and sat in the front of the van.

'What did that man want?' Gustav asked. 'Was he from the authorities?'

'No,' I said. 'He was a businessman.'

'We have to be careful,' said Wolfgang. 'We don't have work permits.'

'Not to worry,' I said. 'Stick with me and you'll be alright.'

A rough count of the completed drums told me we were only about half way through so when the break was over we pressed on as best we could. I was slightly concerned by Kevin and Pete's prolonged absence. For all I knew they might have learnt about the planned changes and simply abandoned us to our fate. When I remembered I was still in possession of their van, however, I realised they would be obliged to return eventually.

As it was they arrived late in the afternoon just when I'd decided to stop work for the day. The gates swung open and the two of them came ambling into the yard.

'Good work,' said Kevin, as he surveyed the scene. 'We've got another batch arriving tomorrow for you to sort out.'

This suited me perfectly because I wanted to keep Gustav and Wolfgang fully occupied for as long as possible. I figured that the more work I found for them the more they would be indebted to me. I'd learnt from Ted Gresham that the current lease expired at the end of the month, which was four days away. That would easily give us time to clear the congestion and leave the yard empty. Installation of the car wash equipment would start a couple of days before the official opening. Obviously I mentioned none of this to Kevin and Pete. They'd already told me it wasn't their yard so really it had nothing to do with them. As long as I got all the drums completed I was sure they would be quite content. Meanwhile, I decided there was no harm in trying to get some more money out of them.

'I presume I'm taking the van again tonight, am I?' I asked.

'Might as well,' said Kevin. 'By the way, why were you late this morning?'

'I've been driving slowly to try and conserve fuel.'

'Oh, don't worry about that. Is the tank empty or something? I can't remember.'

'Could do with a top up.'

'Alright,' he said. 'Tell you what. I'll give you a cheque and you can get some fuel when you've cashed it.'

The thought occurred to me that Kevin was quite free and easy with his cheque book. He dished out cheques willy-nilly as if the bank account was in somebody else's name and not his own. Nonetheless I accepted the cheque he wrote me and put it in my pocket.

'Right,' he said. 'See you here bright and early tomorrow morning.'

After Kevin and Pete had gone I called Gustav and Wolfgang over to the van and we headed for home. We sat side by side with Wolfgang by the window and Gustav in the middle.

'Were you comfortable in your tent last night?' I asked.

'Yes,' said Wolfgang. 'I slept like a log.'

'I didn't,' said Gustav. 'I kept thinking about the damned people who live in this country.'

'Oh, they're not too bad when you get to know them,' I said. 'The only problem is that they're deeply unhappy and nobody knows why.'

'I've got a good idea why,' he replied. 'They've had it far too easy for far too long and they've taken it all for granted.'

Briefly I considered inviting Gustav and Wolfgang to the pub with me that evening so they could meet the locals for themselves. Then maybe Gustav would not be so quick to pass judgement. I swiftly realised, however, that they would require money to buy their beer. I immediately ruled this out because I'd already decided I wasn't going to pay them until the job was completely finished. The alternative was for me to buy all the beers which naturally I had no intention of doing. Also, I didn't think it would be a good idea at this stage if the two of them saw me cashing a cheque: otherwise they'd soon be demanding cheques of their own. In the event, therefore, I chose not to mention the pub at all.

The reason I'd asked how well they'd slept was because there was now only one tent and I was going to have to share with them. They didn't seem to appreciate the sacrifice I was making on their behalf but really I couldn't think of any other solution. Quietly I cursed Harcourt and Kingsnorth for taking away the other tents when my back was turned.

I dropped in at a general store to buy some pre-packed sandwiches and then continued homeward. It was almost dusk when I pulled into the lay-by. The galvanised chain had again been slung between the two posts but fortunately there was no padlock. By now I'd concluded that there was little point in bothering to 'hide' the van overnight so after moving the chain aside I drove right down to the encampment. On arrival I saw that the caravan was still there. Beside it was the pick-up truck I'd seen the night before. I also noticed that the brick hut had been fitted with rafters: apparently someone was planning to put a new roof on it. There was no sign of anybody but a faint light was glowing inside the caravan. I stopped the van by my tent and the three of us got out. Gustav and Wolfgang both announced that they were shattered so after we'd all had some sandwiches they went straight to bed.

A little later the caravan door opened and a man emerged. He acknowledged me with a friendly wave and I wandered over to speak to him.

'Good evening,' he said. 'Much better without the padlock, isn't it?'

'More convenient, yes,' I replied.

'I don't believe in locks and keys.'

'Thought not.'

'You couldn't imagine the amount of times I've had to remove padlocks from that chain.'

'Really?'

'And then they come back and fit a new one. They're always doing it.'

'Who?'

'The railway property board. It's their piece of land. They know I need regular access but they keeping fitting new padlocks. Quite awkward really.'

He now gestured for me to follow him around to the brick hut.

'What do you think of that?' he asked.

In rapidly fading light we stood looking at four brick walls, a broken window, a door and a half-completed roof.

'Well,' I said, 'it certainly has potential.'

'That's what I thought,' said the man. 'I've actually had my eye on it for years but never found time to start work.'

'But now you have?'

'Yes.'

In the back of his pick-up truck were a number of tools, a pane of glass and some timber.

'I run a funfair here once a year,' he explained. 'Barry Barton's Funfair: you've probably seen the notices. There's hardly enough ground space for all the attractions let alone the caravans for my workers so I thought I'd convert this hut into a sort of dormitory. I reckon there's room for three bunk beds inside.'

We peered through the doorway into the gloomy interior.

'What will you do for plumbing?' I enquired.

'Don't need it,' he said. 'There's a standpipe outside the door and all my lads are quite tough.'

'Lights?'

'We'll rig something up.'

It was now too dark to see any more. I thanked him for the guided tour and asked whether he minded us being on the site.

'Not at all,' he said. 'Once I've finished the hut I won't be back until next year and you're bound to have moved on by then. People always do.'

'What about the railway property board?'

'Yes, well, as I mentioned they do tend to be a bit awkward.'

'But surely if you pay them rent they can't keep interfering.'

'I don't pay rent,' he said, 'but I've got long-standing rights. We've been holding funfairs here for decades.'

After informing me that he expected to have the hut ready in a day or two he wished me goodnight and retired to his caravan. I had a wash at the standpipe, changed my clothes and then set off walking briskly to the pub.

When I entered The Wheatsheaf I immediately noticed a change from the previous evening. The place was much busier and around each table were groups of four or five men and women all speaking with their voices lowered. At the end of the bar a man with a microphone was reading out questions which the groups of people were apparently trying to answer. On closer scrutiny I saw that each table had been allocated a sheet of paper and a pencil. Quietly I ordered a pint and asked if I could cash a cheque. After I'd got my beer and my money I went to sit down, only to discover that my usual table had already been taken.

It was occupied by four men who I'd seen in the pub before. They were all quite elderly and appeared to be in the thrall of a gruff-looking character with a pair of spectacles perched on the end of his nose. He was evidently in charge of writing down the answers. I sat at another table nearby.

Eva was on patrol collecting empty glasses. She gave me a nod and a smile as she passed but then put her finger to her lips to indicate I should maintain my silence. This suggested that the event I was witnessing was rather important so I returned her nod and began listening carefully.

Most of the questions I heard were completely baffling and I didn't understand them at all. They dealt mainly with subjects that as a newcomer to the country I couldn't possibly be familiar with. Some questions on the other hand were quite simple and in due course there was one about geography which I knew at once. My neighbours at the next table, however, seemed utterly confounded. All four of them sat shaking their heads and murmuring to one another in an undertone. They were plainly flummoxed so eventually I leaned over and told them the answer. The gruff-looking man waved me away irritably but I was undeterred.

'Believe me,' I said. 'It's definitely correct.'

I repeated the answer a little more assertively.

At that moment a gasp of indignation ran through the entire pub. I heard the microphone being put down with a 'clunk' and then the man asking the questions came stalking across.

'Right, Frank,' he said, addressing the gruff-looking man. 'You're disqualified for accepting outside assistance.'

'Give me a break, Jerry,' came the (gruff) reply. 'We're still debating our answer.'

'Listen, Frank,' said Jerry. 'I'm quizmaster and I have the final say. I'm afraid you're disqualified and that's that.'

The pub then descended into uproar. The quizmaster returned to his station pursued closely by Frank who loudly berated him for his lack of judgment and his blatant bias not to mention the poor quality of his questions. We all heard this because the microphone was still switched on (though their voices were soon lost in a crescendo of feedback). Somebody from another team then got involved and the argument became even more heated. At a nearby table a drink was accidentally knocked over. This led to further recriminations. Meanwhile, Frank's three companions all turned and gave me a hostile stare. In fact, when I looked around the pub I saw that many eyes were upon me. There was much cursing and muttering. I was just beginning to feel a little anxious when all of a sudden the feedback ceased. Frank came marching back to his seat and sat down abruptly. He took up his pencil and in the same instant the voice on the microphone spoke.

'Question eleven,' it said blandly.

Seemingly the quarrel was settled and the quiz was continuing as if nothing had happened.

I finished my pint and wondered if I dared risk ordering another. A second concern was whether Eva had observed the incident. I got my answer when she appeared a minute later with her customary glass of wine and sat down beside me.

'That'll teach you,' she said in a whisper. 'They take their quizzes very seriously.'

'Yes,' I said. 'So I gather.'

'You know why, don't you?'

'No.'

'Life is so comfortable here that they have nothing else to worry about.'

We sat listening in silence as yet more questions were asked and mulled over. I made sure not to offer any help to my neighbours (or anyone else for that matter). After a while Eva told me she had to go back to work.

'Do you ever have a day off?' I enquired.

'Yes,' she said, 'but I spend most of it sleeping.'

I went to the bar and bought a second pint. Half an hour later the quiz ended. When the results were declared it transpired that Frank and his team had won. This came as an immense relief to me. They received a small cash prize plus a free drink for each team member. Shortly after that I slipped quietly out of the pub and headed home. Once again nobody said good night.

9

The following morning I was woken at dawn by a passing train. Immediately I got up and put on my overalls before rousing Gustav and Wolfgang. I wanted to be at the oil drum yard bright and early as commanded by Kevin so I ushered the pair of them into the van and we got going. Our punctual departure meant that we had plenty of time so we stopped for breakfast at Eva's cafe. She was already on duty despite working late in the pub the night before. I was pleased to note that Gustav and Wolfgang kept a respectful silence throughout the meal.

I was equally pleased when we got to the yard before Kevin and Pete. The new batch they'd mentioned had already been delivered but it wasn't a huge amount and I was confident we could get the whole lot finished in a day. When they finally turned up they didn't stay very long. Clearly they'd decided I was quite capable of running the cleaning operation on my own. They said nothing about the imminent takeover of the yard by Ted Gresham and naturally I said nothing either. After they'd left us I allowed a quarter of an hour to elapse before informing Gustav and Wolfgang that I had other business to attend to.

'I should be back by lunchtime,' I said. 'I'll bring some fish and chips.'

I moved the van outside the double gates which I then closed and locked (I didn't want Gustav and Wolfgang going astray while I was absent). As I got back into the van and drove away I was once again overwhelmed with that feeling of empowerment I'd experienced the day before. Here I was behind the wheel of a van with a pocketful of cash and a worthy mission ahead of me. What could be better? I wound down my window and motored along with a warm breeze rushing by.

When I reached the coast road I turned right and continued for several miles. I passed the reception centre and saw the men with placards gathered outside the gate. Evidently they were still on strike. I also noticed a group of tents on a piece of land at the opposite side of the road. I only caught a brief glimpse as I went by but I thought some of them looked slightly familiar. Next moment they were receding in my wing mirror. Ten minutes later I pulled up in a lay-by

a short distance from the seafront. A sign said:
FREE PARKING FOR MAXIMUM OF HALF AN HOUR.

I locked the van and set off towards the beach.

Mr Alder was fairly easy to spot. It was a pleasant day and he was wandering up and down the beach noting the various deckchairs and their occupants. When he'd finished he turned and headed for his hut. A few seconds later the window swung open. I strolled along and found him perched on his stool.

'Morning,' I said.

'Morning,' he replied, reaching for his book of pink tickets. 'Deckchair for one?'

'No thanks.'

'Oh.'

I gave him a broad smile.

'You don't recognise me do you?'

He peered at me closely.

'No,' he said. 'Can't say I do.'

With a flourish I placed my counterfoil before him.

'I've come to pay this fine,' I announced. 'Half a crown I think.'

Mr Alder peered at me with utter incredulity as if I'd just arrived from a remote and distant planet.

'Something the matter?' I enquired.

'Not really,' he managed at length. 'It's just that you're the first person ever to come to this hut and pay their fine. Normally people send a cheque or postal order to county hall.'

'I don't know where that is."

He looked me up and down.

'No,' he said, 'I don't suppose you do.'

Mr Alder was plainly unfamiliar with the procedure for the payment of fines. He fussed around the hut for a few minutes before finding the appropriate book. Then he took the half crown I proffered and gave me a receipt.

'I must admit you're honest,' he remarked. 'Most people in your circumstances wouldn't bother.'

'What circumstances are those then?'

'Well, I've just realised who you are,' he said. 'You're one of the fellows from the boat that sank.'

'Yes I am.'

'Most unfortunate. Looks like a nice boat. It's still there, you know, lying on the sand with the waves breaking over it every day.'

Mr Alder appeared rather saddened by the loss. I wished him good morning and walked down the steps to the beach. I'd decided that while I was here I might as well check on the condition of the boat. The tide was out at present so I'd be able to give it a proper inspection. Maybe there was still a chance it could be salvaged after all. As I approached the breakwater where we'd left the boat I saw a man standing gazing out to sea. I recognised Kingsnorth immediately and called his name. When he turned and saw who it was he didn't look very pleased to see me.

'Hello, Kingsnorth,' I said, walking up. 'What are you doing here?'

'I've come to check on the boat,' he replied.

'Yes, and me.'

It lay before us covered in a coating of wet sand which we brushed off to reveal the holes drilled by the vandals. I imagined that in competent hands the boat was most probably repairable. For the time being, however, it would have to remain at the mercy of the elements.

'Still cleaning those oil drums?' Kingsnorth asked.

'Yes,' I said. 'We've got face masks now.'

'Well, that's an improvement.'

'Actually I'll be moving out of oil drums very soon.'

'Oh yes?'

'I'm starting a new venture that you might be interested in.'

When he heard this Kingsnorth treated me to a sceptical gaze. Plainly he wasn't interested so I decided to change the subject.

'How did you and Harcourt get on at the reception centre?'

'We're still there,' said Kingsnorth. 'We've established a protest camp right opposite.'

Apparently he and Harcourt had reached the conclusion that the only way any progress could be made was to draw public attention to the strike: hence the protest camp. He told me they'd already attracted several new adherents. In turn I recounted what had happened on the night they thought I'd abandoned them. The explanation seemed to mollify him a little and he became less prickly.

'Are you going back to the reception centre now?' I enquired.

'That's the intention,' said Kingsnorth.

'I can give you a lift if you like,' I said. 'I've still got the van: it'll save you having to walk.'

I then realised that my half hour had nearly expired. Swiftly the pair of us hurried back to the lay-by. When we reached the van Kingsnorth cast a critical eye over it. A particular item had caught his attention.

'Aha,' he said. 'The ubiquitous red and white flag.'

'Yes, I've noticed it's quite popular,' I replied.

We were soon on our way to the reception centre. As we approached I saw that there were five tents in the protest camp. Above them fluttered a banner that said simply: HOW LONG MUST WE WAIT? I pulled up nearby and we got out of the van. Several men and women emerged from the various tents. Among them was Harcourt. He came and joined Kingsnorth and me. We greeted one another and then I peered across the road at the strikers.

'Any progress in their dispute?' I enquired.

'I'm afraid not,' said Harcourt. 'The two parties seem to be at absolute loggerheads.'

'How have they been treating you?'

'Not too bad actually. We've made friends with some of the men on the gate. They told us they feel they have more in common with us than with their employers. They even brought over a tea urn for us to use.'

'And some biscuits,' Kingsnorth reminded him.

'Ah, yes,' said Harcourt. 'Malted Milk. Very nice indeed.'

He went on to outline a plan he'd recently conceived. He proposed to offer his services as arbitrator between the two sides. He admitted it was a long shot but at least it was worth trying.

'It's a shame the way people in this country constantly squabble amongst themselves,' he said. 'They can't even agree on general principles let alone minor details. They're forever at each other's throats. Rather tragic actually.'

I was glad to see Harcourt's altruistic self coming to the fore once again. At the same time it struck me that my own efforts had recently been diverted from such high moral standards. We'd come here to help these people yet I'd swiftly become engaged in a number of less righteous practises. I pictured the squalor of the oil drum yard where Gustav and Wolfgang were currently hard at work behind locked gates. All of a sudden I realised I'd forgotten all about their fish and chips! I'd promised them several hours ago and by now they must be desperate!

In a state of panic I said goodbye to Harcourt and Kingsnorth before leaping into the van and speeding away. When I looked in my wing mirror I saw the cameras at the reception centre swinging around to focus on my registration plate. It was too late to do anything about it now so I just kept going.

By the time I'd collected the fish and chips (plus some fizzy drinks) and got back to the yard it was early afternoon. The double gates were still locked so quickly I opened them and peeped inside. Both Gustav and Wolfgang were sitting on the stack of plastic sacks looking very sorry for themselves. They appeared to have completed a good few drums, however, so I marched in and announced my return.

'Now for a well-deserved break,' I declared breezily. 'Luncheon is served.'

Despite the generous portions (I'd ordered extra chips and mushy peas) the two of them were clearly aggrieved. They sat in morose silence as they devoured their mountainous meals and spoke neither to each other or me. For my part I was glad that they'd managed to work all morning uninterrupted. If Kevin and Pete had happened to drop by during my absence I would have had a lot of explaining to do. As it was I could see we were in a strong position to wind the job up before nightfall if we kept hard at it. With this in mind I allowed Gustav and Wolfgang another fifteen minutes of rest before strolling across to the completed drums.

'Right,' I said. 'I'll get these stacked up and you two can carry on as you were.'

'Will we be getting paid soon?' Gustav enquired.

'Yes, should be tonight if we get this job finished.'

Seemingly I'd offered sufficient incentive to get them moving again and we had another very productive afternoon. The light was beginning to fade when finally the last half a dozen drums joined the stack. Once again the yard was flowing with effluent as we climbed into the van and waited for Kevin and Pete to return.

'Probably won't be long,' I said. 'They generally turn up at the end of the working day.'

Even as I spoke I had an uneasy feeling that actually they wouldn't turn up. On previous occasions they'd habitually arrived about an hour before dusk but today there was no sign of them. The feeling worsened as darkness continued to fall and eventually I gave up waiting.

'Have to try and catch them tomorrow,' I affirmed, trying to adopt an optimistic tone.

'Well, can't we have some money anyway?' said Gustav. 'You did say you'd pay us tonight if we got the job finished.'

'You don't understand,' I said. 'I've got to wait until they pay me.'

'But I saw Kevin give you a cheque yesterday.'

'That was to buy fuel.'

The statement was technically true, of course. Nevertheless I was coming to realise that I couldn't prevaricate for very much longer.

Gustav and Wolfgang had fulfilled their end of the bargain and completed the work. Furthermore, I knew I needed to maintain a certain degree of trust if I was going to transfer them onto Ted Gresham's workforce at the car wash. I was actually quite flush with money because I was still holding Harcourt and Kingsnorth's earnings in reserve. Therefore with some reluctance I reached into my pocket.

'When I go and cash a cheque,' I said, 'it's discounted at a rate of twenty five per cent.'

I went on to explain to Gustav and Wolfgang that I would have to charge them the same rate of discount. I also pointed out that there were certain other deductions I was obliged to make as well. When I was satisfied they both had a full grasp of the financial situation I gave them each some banknotes and we then set off back to the fairground. On arrival I saw in the headlights that the pick-up truck and caravan had now departed. We seemingly had the place to ourselves again.

After Gustav and Wolfgang had settled into the tent for the evening I went back to the van and searched in the glove compartment. I was sure I'd seen Pete put his torch in there and sure enough I soon found it. I thought it would be interesting to see how the improvements to the brick hut were proceeding. By torchlight I carried out an inspection and I had to admit I was highly impressed. Barry Barton obviously knew what he was doing. The roof had been fully repaired with sheets of corrugated iron and there was a new pane of glass in the window frame. When I tried the door I discovered it wasn't locked. This came as no surprise: I remembered him mentioning that he didn't believe in locks and keys. When I shone my torch inside I saw three newly-constructed bunk beds. The chimney from the cast iron stove protruded neatly through a sealed aperture in the roof. There was even a new wooden floor. In short, he'd transformed the former railwayman's hut into a tiny little home from home.

Without a second thought I went over to the tent and retrieved my bedding. Gustav and Wolfgang were already fast asleep and I hoped they would appreciate the extra space I was allowing them. I returned to the hut and changed out of my overalls before settling on the upper bunk in the corner. My plan was to have a brief doze and then go to the pub later. I had no new cheque to cash but after the incident during the quiz I wanted to make sure I was still welcome. There was also the prospect of maybe seeing Eva.

It turned out, however, that I was more tired than I realised. No sooner had I closed my eyes than I, too, fell into a deep sleep. When next I awoke there was daylight streaming in through the window. It took me a moment to remember where I was exactly. I knew I didn't have to get up and go to work but then it dawned on me that I needed to track down Kevin and Pete fairly soon. I got out of the bunk and went outside to wash at the standpipe. There was no sign of Gustav and Wolfgang so I presumed they were still asleep. This suited me fine as I didn't want the complication of having them tagging along with me. Especially not today.

I decided that my first port of call had to be the oil drum yard. There was a distinct possibility that Kevin and Pete weren't avoiding me at all. Perhaps they'd merely been delayed somewhere the previous evening. In that case they would no doubt go directly to the yard at the earliest opportunity to check how the work was progressing. Once they'd seen for themselves that the job had been completed they'd pay me the balance and that would be that. Besides which, of course, I still had possession of their van. They were bound to want it back eventually.

Arriving at the yard half an hour later I saw that the double gates were wide open. I stopped at the side of the road. A flatbed lorry was parked in the gateway and some men I hadn't seen before were loading the finished oil drums onto it. The lorry was flying the usual red and white flag. There was a man standing apart from the others. He was directing operations and when he spotted me he came marching over to the van.

'Morning,' he said. 'Are you Ted Gresham's new business associate?'

'Er…yes,' I said. 'Sort of.'

'Oh, right,' he said. 'Well, I've heard you're taking on men for this new car wash you're opening.'

'Yes, we are.'

'It's just that I'm going to have to lay off a few of my blokes until I get another yard sorted out. I forgot all about the lease expiring and it's left me in an awkward position. Do you think you could do me a favour and give them a try for a week or two?'

'How many altogether?'

'Three.'

'Should be alright,' I said. 'We're always looking for reliable people.'

He lowered his voice.

'I can guarantee they're reliable,' he said, 'although strictly speaking they're not supposed to be working if you see what I mean. It'll be cash only. No questions asked and I'll take them back as soon as I'm fixed up.'

'What if I want to keep them?'

'We'll worry about that when the time comes.'

I explained to him that there was a non-refundable recruitment premium of ten percent and he agreed at once. We also agreed that the men should turn up at the car wash the day before it opened so they could be shown the ropes. I told him the scheduled date, then we shook hands on the deal and he thanked me profusely. (I'd come to notice that if people in this country said 'thank you' they always said it quite profusely as if they were tipping an imaginary cap to someone of higher social status. In fact they said 'thank you' so frequently it almost sounded like an apology.) As he walked away I peered at his lorry and saw the words BOB TWIGG: NO JOB TOO SMALL stencilled on the side of the cab along with a telephone number.

By now I was ready for breakfast so I set off towards the cafe. With luck I would find Kevin and Pete there and we could get matters settled. When I thought about it properly, however, it struck me that a little caution wouldn't go amiss. For this reason I parked the van about half a mile from the cafe behind a do-it-yourself emporium. With the keys safely in my pocket I walked the rest of the way.

I was half-disappointed, half-relieved when I entered the cafe and discovered that Kevin and Pete weren't there. The eggs, chips and beans table was empty but there were plenty of other customers including four men in identical yellow and green boiler suits. They all had hearty breakfasts in front of them. I went and sat at a table by the window and after a while Eva came and took my order.

'Eggs, chips and beans?' she enquired.

I felt she was gently mocking me so I chose a cheese and tomato omelette instead.

'Just to be adventurous,' I remarked.

She nodded and left me alone.

Not long afterwards the door swung open and Kevin and Pete walked in. I could at tell at once that they weren't expecting to see me but they covered it quite well and greeted me warmly like a long lost friend. They even came and sat at the same table.

'Already ordered, have you?' Pete asked.

'Yes, thanks. Cheese and tomato omelette.'

'Good idea,' he said and when Eva returned he ordered the same for both of them.

'Suppose you're after some money,' said Kevin.

'Well, it would help,' I said, 'and we did finish the job.'

He nodded gravely.

'The trouble is,' he said, 'we're having a bit of a cash flow problem at present. We're going to pay you in due course but we just haven't got it yet.'

'What about a cheque?'

'I'm afraid the cheque book's empty.'

'And we haven't had the chance to order a new one,' added Pete quickly.

At this moment Eva placed three mugs of tea on the table along with our bread and butter.

'Sorry about this,' said Kevin. 'It's just the way it is.'

'When do you think you'll have some money?' I asked.

'Not sure,' he said. 'Possibly a couple of weeks.'

'Well, is it alright if I hold onto the van in the meantime?'

Kevin and Pete both gave me a look of mild surprise. Clearly the idea hadn't occurred to either of them. Just then our omelettes arrived so I put salt and pepper on mine while they quietly conferred.

'Tell you what,' said Kevin at length, 'you can have our other van if you want.'

'What's the difference?' I asked.

'Yours has got a sliding door on the side. The other one hasn't.'

'And you need a sliding door?'

'It'll be handy for our next job, yes.'

I'd only seen the other van once and I'd barely glanced at it let alone notice the lack of a sliding door. It was only a minor detail but clearly Kevin and Pete viewed it as important. Personally speaking I wasn't really bothered. To my mind it was just a van.

'Alright,' I said. 'That sounds fair enough. I'll go and fetch it after breakfast.'

'Where is it anyway?' said Pete. 'We didn't see it outside.'

'I parked it somewhere else.'

'Why?'

'I wasn't sure if I'd get a space here.'

The pair of them regarded me quizzically.

'But there are always spaces here.'

'Maybe so,' I said, 'but I couldn't be certain.'

Fortunately they didn't pursue the matter further and instead focused on their omelettes. Eventually breakfast was concluded and Eva brought us our second teas. At some stage I expected either Kevin or Pete to mention the forthcoming closure of the oil drum yard but again they said nothing. We sat in contemplative silence for a few minutes and then I announced that I would go and get the van.

'I'll be about a quarter of an hour.'

'Okay,' said Kevin. 'We'll wait here.'

I walked back to the do-it-yourself emporium feeling fairly satisfied with the way the morning had gone. Not only had I made the deal with Bob Twigg but I now also had short term possession of my own van. I was quite confident that I would eventually extract some more money from Kevin and Pete and meanwhile I could begin putting together a workforce for Ted Gresham.

As I crossed the car park at the do-it-yourself emporium I saw that there was a sheet of paper tucked under the van's windscreen wipers. It bore a slight resemblance to the parking ticket that Eva had issued so with some concern I opened it to read what it said. The note stated that the vehicle had incurred a penalty for parking on private land. It pointed out that the designated parking spaces were solely for the use of customers. Consequently the vehicle's owner would in due course receive a demand by post. In case of doubt the incident had been recorded on camera. I folded the note and put it in my pocket before driving back to the cafe.

10

Kevin and Pete had been having a think.

'We've been having a think,' said Kevin when I rejoined them at the table.

'Oh yes?'

'We propose letting you have the van in full settlement of what we owe you.'

'You mean the other van?'

'Yeah.'

'Why's that then?'

'Well, we've been planning to downsize our operation for a while and this seems an opportune moment.'

I pondered the offer.

'I presume it's in good condition.'

'Of course,' Kevin replied. 'You can go and give it a once over if you like. It's right outside the door.'

With that he placed a bunch of keys on the table. In the same instant I realised he was setting me a challenge. If I took the keys to go and inspect the van I'd be implying that I didn't quite trust his word. This in turn could be interpreted as an insult. On the other hand if I didn't check the vehicle and it turned out to be faulty I'd have only myself to blame. Eventually I decided on a compromise. In reality there was no point in me looking under the bonnet because I knew nothing about engines. Therefore I left the keys on the table and went outside. I then walked around the van kicking the tyres and running my hands over the paintwork before going back inside the cafe and sitting down opposite Kevin and Pete.

'Seems okay,' I said.

'Right,' said Kevin. 'Here you are then.'

He pushed the bunch of keys across the table towards me and at the same time I put my set in front of him.

'Obviously we'll be in touch if we need your help again,' said Pete, 'but for the time being you're surplus to requirements.'

Shortly afterwards the two of them departed. I caught Eva's eye and ordered another mug of tea. I now had a day or two of spare time before the car wash opened so there was no need for me to go hurrying off. Instead, I sat back in my chair and absorbed the general ambience of the cafe. It had now emptied considerably since the morning rush and the only remaining customers apart from me were the four men in the yellow and green boiler suits. They appeared to be in no particular hurry to leave. Each of them had a mug of tea and they were all engaged in some lively banter which was difficult not to overhear.

Their van was parked outside the cafe directly in front of mine. Both vehicles flew identical red and white flags and this told me they were fellow countrymen of Kevin and Pete. Even so they struck me as being entirely different types. I'd seen for myself how crafty Kevin and Pete were with all their wheeling and dealing whereas these four came over as very straightforward characters. Even their way of speaking was different. Kevin and Pete both spoke in a sharp sort of way while these men intoned their words much more flatly. Another noticeable trait was that they frequently spoke of 'back home' and 'down here' which suggested they weren't originally from this region. Moreover the tea they were drinking was apparently inferior to what they were used to. (They stressed that this was not the fault of the cafe: rather it was the quality of the water.)

Nonetheless they unanimously decided on another mug apiece.

Judging from their conversation I gathered that they would much prefer to be in their home territory (wherever that was). I wondered if this sense of displacement contributed to the pervasive national despondency that my comrades and I had come to try and help cure. Under closer scrutiny, however, the hypotheses fell at the first hurdle because the four men were markedly cheerful. As a matter of fact they seemed to revel in their situation: it was almost as though they were thoroughly enjoying their homesickness and nobody was going to deprive them of it.

The more I listened to them the more nonplussed I became. How on earth were we going to help these unhappy people when they wouldn't even admit they were unhappy? When finally they left the cafe they all individually said goodbye to me after profusely thanking Eva and the rest of the staff (including an unseen person toiling somewhere in the depths of the kitchen).

Not long after they'd gone Eva brought me a mug of tea (seemingly 'on the house') and sat down at my table.

'I see you've got yourself another van,' she remarked.

'Yes,' I said, 'though I haven't actually driven it yet.'

She smiled.

'Oh, well, there's always a first time for everything.'

She toyed distractedly with the salt cellar and I began to get the feeling she was working towards something. This suited me fine because as far as I was concerned the longer she sat there the better.

'So you're planning to open a car wash,' she said at length.

'How on earth do you know that?' I asked.

'They were all talking about it at the eggs, chips and beans table yesterday.'

'Really?'

'I heard it mentioned several times.'

'Yes, well, I dare say a bit of free publicity won't do any harm and naturally they'll be very welcome to bring their cars over once we get going.'

'Oh, I don't think any of them own a car,' she said. 'Not on the eggs, chips and beans table.'

'No, I suppose not.'

'They wanted to know if there are any jobs.'

'There might be.'

'They said you were in charge of recruitment.'

'Yes, I am.'

'Well, could you do me a favour?'

'Of course.'

'Could you give my boyfriend a job?'

Needless to say the request hit me like a sledgehammer. I'd been sitting there trying to impress Eva with my influential new role and now it had backfired on me. The thought had simply never occurred to me that she might be involved with somebody. I'd just assumed she was alone in a foreign land like I was. Now she'd got me well and truly boxed in.

I thought for a moment.

'I don't suppose you can get that parking ticket cancelled?' I enquired.

'No, sorry,' said Eva. 'I'm afraid not.'

She gazed at me without expression. I had no idea what she truly thought of me but I really didn't want to fall out of her esteem.

'Alright, tell him to be at the oil drum yard at eight o'clock the day after tomorrow.'

'He hasn't got any transport.'
'Well, where does he live?'
'In the flat upstairs. Same as me.'
'Okay, I'll pick him up at half past seven.'
'Thanks.'

She gave me another smile before leaving the table to resume her work. I finished my tea and left the cafe with a cheery 'goodbye' but deep inside I felt decidedly peeved. When I climbed into the van and started the engine I noticed immediately that the milometer said almost 99000 miles (the other van had scarcely done half that). Moreover, the fuel tank was virtually empty. This meant that as soon as I commenced my journey back to the fairground I had to start looking for a filling station. Hitherto I'd paid little attention to the price of fuel in this country and it came as quite a shock when ten minutes later I pulled in beside a pump. As I parted with a large quantity of carefully-accumulated money I realised my situation wasn't nearly as rosy as it had seemed a few hours earlier.

When finally I arrived at the fairground I saw that Gustav and Wolfgang had taken down the remaining tent and folded it away.

'Thinking of leaving?' I enquired.

'No,' said Gustav. 'We noticed that you'd moved your bedding into that brick hut in the corner.'

'Yes,' I said. 'Correct.'

'We'd like to do the same.'

'Don't you like sleeping in the tent then?'

'It's bearable,' he replied, 'but you know as well as we do that a proper roof is significantly better.'

I really didn't like Gustav's manner of speaking. At the same time, however, I saw an opportunity to recoup some of my recent losses.

'Well, I'm using the hut by special arrangement with the owner,' I said. 'It belongs to the railway property board.'

'Yes, we know,' he said. 'We've been making enquiries.'

'Who with?'

'There were some railwaymen working on the embankment this morning. We asked them.'

'Maybe you did but they're probably unaware of the special arrangement.'

He slowly shook his head.

'No,' he admitted, 'nothing was said about that.'

I felt I'd scored a minor victory over him so now was the time to show some magnanimity.

'I didn't have time to tell you this morning but, yes, you're quite welcome to move in and join me.'

'Thank you,' murmured Gustav.

'Obviously I'll need to deduct a certain amount of rent from your wages.'

I could see that he was about to raise an objection but fortunately Wolfgang interposed.

'So you have some more work lined up for us?' he said hopefully.

'Yes,' I said, 'and it's a lot better than cleaning oil drums. Starting the day after tomorrow you'll be washing cars for a living.'

My announcement lifted the mood considerably and for the time being I received no further demands from Gustav. Even so I knew I was going to have to keep him firmly in check.

'Have you both got some money left?' I asked.

'Yes,' said Wolfgang. 'We've had nothing to spend it on.'

'Right, well, how would you like a visit to the pub tonight?'

'What?' Gustav sneered. 'And mingle with the populace? No thanks.'

'But you'll have to meet them sooner or later,' I pointed out.

'Well, I think I'll defer that pleasure for as long as possible if you don't mind.'

'I'll come,' said Wolfgang.

So it was that the two of us set off in the van about half an hour later. I'd decided that it would be a strict two-pinter and therefore I was safe to drive there and back. At the top of the concrete road I took care to sling the galvanised chain between the two posts and then we headed into the night. The pub, when we arrived, was fairly empty. I guided Wolfgang towards the corner table and then went to buy some drinks. As I approached the bar Norman was already filling a glass with my usual.

'No cheque tonight?'

'No,' I said. 'Just the beer please. Two pints actually.'

'Right you are.'

I rejoined Wolfgang nonchalantly assuming I had a peaceful evening ahead of me. We hardly knew one another so I thought we might exchange a few niceties and that would be it. I swiftly learnt, however, that his idea of a conversation was to bombard me with a stream of questions. He began by asking about the car wash so I gave him a few details without divulging too much information. He then went on to enquire how I'd discovered the fairground. Once I'd gone through that he wanted to know all about Kevin and Pete, about the factory and ultimately about Harcourt, Kingsnorth and the rest of them. I had no doubt that the next on the list would be Eva. Wolfgang seemed to have no concept of sitting in a pub quietly enjoying a beer for its own sake. Instead, whenever there was a period of silence he would merely dream up another question. In due course we both finished our drinks. Our glasses stood empty on the table for a good five minutes while I waited patiently for him to go and buy another round. Yet he remained sitting where he was.

'That waitress in the cafe,' he said. 'What's her name?'

'Eva.'

'An acquaintance of yours?'

'Yes.'

'Do you know her very well?'

'No.'

'Would you like to know her better?'

'Look Wolfgang!' I snapped. 'You have to learn that if somebody buys you a drink you should buy them one in return!'

'Oh, sorry, I didn't realise,' he said. 'Is it a custom in this country?'

'Yes, I think it is.'

'But you're not from this country are you?'

At this moment a voice called from behind the bar. It belonged to Norman who'd apparently been observing my torment.

'Two pints here,' he said, 'when you're ready.'

I gave Wolfgang a nod and he obediently went up to the bar. There was a slight delay as he fished out his money (it was in a hidden pocket) and then he returned with the drinks.

'There you are,' I remarked. 'Easy wasn't it?'

I slightly regretted being so harsh with Wolfgang but I told myself the lesson wouldn't do him any harm in the long run. The real reason I was irked, needless to say, was because he'd asked about Eva. It was evidently her night off from the pub and I guessed she was out on her moped issuing parking tickets. This was confirmed a little later when the woman with the multiple earrings emerged from the saloon bar and began collecting empty glasses. Wolfgang had no inkling about Eva's job in The Wheatsheaf so naturally I didn't mention it. Otherwise it was likely to trigger a further round of questioning. Now that I had my pint in my hand I was able to be a bit nicer to him and the rest of the evening passed agreeably enough.

When finally we left the pub we were both rewarded with a 'good night' from Norman. We got back in the van and returned to the fairground without incident. On arrival we found that in our absence Gustav had already moved into the brick hut. He was lying fast asleep in the dark. I then remembered that the torch was in the other van. As a consequence Wolfgang and I had to feel our way into our respective bunks while trying not to wake him. Once we were settled down I quietly reminded Wolfgang that he and Gustav had a free day tomorrow.

'What will you be doing?' he asked.

'I'm going along to the reception centre to see if there have been any developments.'

'Oh, right.'

'You've both got money in your pockets,' I said, 'so you'll have to fend for yourselves until I return.'

11

My first stop next morning was the general store. I bought a new padlock as well as a few other supplies before proceeding towards the coast. I'd learnt from experience not to take the van anywhere near the reception centre so when there was still about a mile to go I pulled into a lay-by that said FREE PARKING ALL DAY. I then completed the rest of the journey on foot.

As soon as I drew near I saw that the protest camp had enlarged somewhat since my previous visit. I counted at least twelve tents as well as a few dilapidated dormobiles (some of them painted in gaudy colours). Several men and women were wandering among them and at the far side of the camp a brazier was smouldering. Standing around it were Harcourt, Kingsnorth and several of the strikers from the gate. My immediate impression was that they were all great friends. They were laughing and joking and when I joined them I was offered a mug of tea from the urn.

'Glad to see you've got rid of that damned van,' said Harcourt. 'A veritable symbol of exploitation.'

'Yes,' I replied. 'I more or less gave it away.'

'And now you've come to support us?'

'For an hour or so, yes.'

I was then introduced to a man called Derek who described himself as the strike coordinator. He informed me that the dispute was taking a turn for the worst because the management had started bussing untrained personnel into the reception centre. This was to enable a new system of fast-tracking to be inaugurated.

'Only a matter of days,' he said, 'and they'll begin processing people again.'

'Catastrophic,' muttered Harcourt.

'But surely that'll help you,' I said, 'if it means you'll be dealt with sooner.'

'No, no, no, you don't understand,' Derek interjected. 'They call it 'fast-tracking' but really they're just cutting corners.'

'Oh, I see.'

'We have to stand shoulder to shoulder with Derek and his colleagues,' Harcourt announced. 'Correct procedures must be maintained at all times.'

'But they'll still be processing people,' I ventured. 'What's the difference?'

'Because properly trained personnel do it properly,' intoned Derek. 'That's what they're trained for.'

He finished his tea, gave me a curt nod and then crossed the road to the gate where a dozen or so men stood holding placards.

'I offered my services as arbitrator,' said Harcourt.

'Any luck?' I asked.

'The management didn't even bother to reply.'

'Nice of them.'

'So now I know whose side I'm on.'

I peered towards the reception centre.

'The untrained personnel,' I said. 'Are they in there now?'

'Yes,' replied Harcourt. 'They were bussed in quite early this morning.'

'Any idea where from?'

'Can't be certain,' he said, 'but somebody mentioned they came from north of the border.'

'I didn't know they had internal borders in this country.'

'There are several actually.'

'So presumably the people who were bussed in have already been processed themselves.'

'You mean by other officials?'

'Yes.'

'I suppose they must have been,' said Harcourt with a frown. 'I hadn't thought of that.'

He pondered in silence for a moment.

'The problems that beset this nation,' he continued at length, 'are practically innumerable. Nobody will admit it but their society is completely tangled with many overlapping layers of identity, allegiance and sense of belonging. It'll never change because they just cover it up with a smile and a wave. Do you know it's against the law here to ask somebody where they come from?'

'Why?'

'In case it causes offence.'

'But that's preposterous.'

'Indeed.'

While we'd been talking we'd been quietly joined by a woman from the protest camp. She waited unobtrusively until we'd finished our conversation and then asked if I'd like some lunch.

'That's kind of you,' I said. 'Thanks.'

She told me her name was Tamara and led me across to a marquee. Inside was a wooden trestle table laden with food and beverages. Several other people were seated on benches. Tamara told me to help myself to whatever I liked so I loaded up a tray before sitting down to eat.

'Are you having anything yourself?' I enquired.

'No,' she replied. 'My job's just to get people in here.'

'Ah.'

'You look as though you have a very healthy appetite.'

'Do I?'

'More than most people anyway.'

I glanced around and saw that each of my fellow diners had selected just a single item from the trestle table, whereas my tray was full to capacity. I then noticed a sign requesting voluntary contributions towards the food and drink that had been generously donated in support of the protest camp.

'No hurry,' remarked Tamara. 'Enjoy.'

She smiled and left me alone.

Personally I couldn't see much chance of the protest succeeding. As I understood it they were trying to draw attention to the fact that the reception centre was closed due to strike action. This precept was obviously flawed. Harcourt and his adherents seemed to think that the eventual reopening of the centre would allow them access to the country through the proper channels. Maybe so but there was an equal chance they could be courting disaster. The reception centre was there for a reason and I didn't think it was a particularly welcoming one. Quite the opposite actually. The fact was that 'processing' didn't necessarily mean 'acceptance'. For all Harcourt knew there might be very strict rules involved. Moreover, to judge by the enduring nature of the strike the people who ran the centre were sharply divided amongst themselves. This was bound to be reflected in the way they carried out their work. A discontented employee could easily put a cross in a box where there should really be a tick.

Then there was the question of the camp's burgeoning population. I suspected that Tamara wasn't from these shores but nevertheless she appeared highly accomplished in her 'front of house' role. As a fully-assimilated individual she was presumably protesting on behalf of those less fortunate than herself. The presence of some of the other newcomers was less easy to explain. The majority didn't look as if they'd just arrived by boat (especially not the ones with dormobiles) and it occurred to me that they might simply be searching for something to protest against. This in itself could cause complications. The purpose of the camp was to win potential supporters but if it continued to expand it was just as likely to provoke the wrath of the department of sanitation. Harcourt would no doubt find a solution to such problems but that wasn't the point. He really needed to take control of matters before they got out of hand.

When I left the marquee I made sure Tamara observed me putting my 'contribution' in the collection box. I then went and said goodbye to Harcourt and Kingsnorth before heading homeward. Neither of them asked how

I'd been occupying myself since we'd last met so I didn't bother telling them. They were both so engrossed with the minutiae of the dispute that nothing else was of interest. I wished them luck and set off walking back to the van.

I'd only gone a short distance when a vehicle pulled in beside me.

'Can I give you a lift anywhere?'

It was Tamara. She was sitting behind the wheel of a multi-coloured dormobile.

'Well, I haven't got far to go,' I said. 'I don't mind walking.'

'How far?'

'About a mile.'

'Hop in,' she said. 'I'll give you a ride.'

Tamara had apparently never heard of speed restrictions. She drove that dormobile so fast that barely two minutes later we arrived at the lay-by and she dropped me off. We'd have got there even sooner if it hadn't been for a couple of pairs of traffic lights (both on red). During the brief pauses she told me that volunteering at the protest camp was only what she did on her day off. She was also holding down two paid jobs.

'There's so much work available in this country,' she said, 'but they can't find anyone to do it.'

'No,' I said, 'I've noticed that.'

'There used to be a scheme for full employment: all properly regulated with fixed hours of work and fixed rates of pay.'

'Sounds good.'

'Fizzled out years ago. These days it's a free-for-all.'

Our conversation was only brief but after she'd sped away I regretted not making more effort to remain in touch.

I got into the van and sat thinking about what lay ahead. Clearly the following day would be rather hectic. Ted Gresham was expecting me at the yard and I hoped it would all go smoothly. Not only would I be in charge of Gustav and Wolfgang but I would be meeting up with Bob Twigg's three former employees for the first time. Also, of course, I had to collect Eva's boyfriend from outside the cafe. The thought of this was particularly unpalatable but really I felt I had no choice but to go along with it. I also decided that because tomorrow required an early start there would be no visit to The Wheatsheaf tonight.

I put the van in gear and got moving.

It was late afternoon when the railway arch appeared ahead of me. I turned off the main road, passed between the two posts and then stopped to fit the new padlock onto the galvanised chain. Now that we'd taken up permanent residence at the fairground it seemed a good idea to deter unwanted visitors: hence the padlock.

As I continued down the concrete road I wondered what Gustav and Wolfgang had been doing during their free day. I soon found out.

Fluttering on a pole above the brick hut was a large flag that I vaguely recognised. There was smoke issuing from the chimney and Gustav and Wolfgang were sitting on the doorstep waving at passing trains.

I stopped and got out of the van.

'What's that flag doing there?' I demanded.

'It's our national flag,' replied Gustav. 'We always carry it with us.'

'You're meant to be keeping a low profile not attracting attention.'

'I thought you said you had a special arrangement with the railway property board.'

'I have,' I said, 'but it doesn't include flagpoles and coal fires.'

'It's wood actually,' said Wolfgang. 'The evenings have been turning chilly and we wanted to keep warm.'

I peered inside the brick hut and saw that the pair of them had taken over two of the bunk beds. There was clothing hanging all over the place though my own bunk remained empty. A pile of sticks lay beside the cast iron stove.

'Well, I suppose the smoke is innocuous enough,' I said, 'but the flag will definitely have to come down.'

'That seems highly unfair,' said Gustav.

'It's nothing to do with fairness. Just common sense.'

'But we see other people flying those red and white flags all the time,' he said. 'Why shouldn't we fly ours?'

'Because I say so!' I snapped. 'If you don't take it down I'll take it down for you and you can forget about working at the car wash! I can easily get other people!'

Reluctantly he took down the flag and folded it away. On close inspection I found that they'd made the pole from a piece of timber left behind by Barry Barton. This, too, I ordered to be taken down. A few minutes later a train went by on the embankment above us. Neither Gustav nor Wolfgang waved to the passengers.

I was now acutely aware of the resentment they felt towards me but I was determined not to give way to them. I enquired if they'd eaten and they confirmed that they had.

'We walked a mile or so to some shops,' said Wolfgang. 'We spent most of our money.'

'Well, you'll be earning again once the car wash gets started,' I said. 'I've secured you a very reasonable rate.'

'And I suppose you'll be taking your cut,' said Gustav.

'Of course.'

Soon darkness was beginning to fall. We passed a quiet evening feeding sticks into the cast iron stove and watching them crackle in the flames. Later I went for a brief stroll up the concrete road and back. The purpose was merely to stretch my legs so that I'd sleep better when I went to bed.

As I approached the galvanised chain I noticed the flash of a torch ahead of me. I stopped in my tracks. For a moment I faintly hoped that Eva had come to pay me a visit. Such ideas were swiftly dashed, however, when I heard men's voices. They uttered a few words and then the torchlight began moving away. I waited half a minute and heard doors slamming and an engine starting. Quickly I moved through the shadows to try and catch a glimpse of the vehicle. In the gloom I saw that it was a van with some words stencilled on the side: RAILWAY PROPERTY BOARD. I watched as it pulled out of the lay-by and drove into the night.

Once I was certain the van had gone I checked the padlock and discovered it was still in place. I was now in a quandary as to whether to leave it there or not. Anybody could see that we had staked a claim on the fairground but it was unclear if the property board would take further action. I had no idea if the padlock could be interpreted as evidence of trespass or else an assertion of long-standing rights. Still, the matter was out of my hands now because the bird had already flown.

I returned to the brick hut and found Gustav and Wolfgang lying in their bunks.

'Right,' I said. 'Early start tomorrow.'

Neither of them replied. They simply turned on their sides and went to sleep.

The fire in the stove had gone out when I awoke next morning. I rolled out of bed and opened the door. It looked like a fine day so I gave Gustav and Wolfgang a nudge each and went outside. A couple of minutes later they emerged from the hut.

'What about breakfast?' Gustav enquired.

'We'll have some later,' I said. 'We need to get going fairly soon so can the two of you please hurry up?'

Despite their argumentative ways I'd learnt that they both responded quite well to firm discipline. In consequence we were in the van and away by seven o'clock. Gustav made no comment when I asked him to remove the padlock and replace it after we'd passed through. He and Wolfgang merely sat in silence as we headed onto the main road and began our journey. Nothing was said for the next half hour. There was a radio in the van but it didn't work. The only sound was the clamour of the engine.

I hadn't told Gustav and Wolfgang that we were making an additional stop so naturally when we drew near the cafe they assumed I'd changed my mind about breakfast. I heard murmurs of anticipation coming from the seats beside me and I started to explain that they would have to wait a little longer.

'I want to go to the car wash first,' I said, 'so that you can learn the ropes. After that we'll come back and have a proper breakfast.'

Just then a figure appeared at the side of the road. I guessed this was Eva's boyfriend so I slowed down and pulled over.

To my profound disbelief I saw that it was Johnson.

12

When he noticed me behind the wheel of the van he looked equally surprised. He was wearing the same yellow and green boiler suit as the four men I'd seen in the cafe a few days earlier. There was no sliding door on the side of the vehicle so I told Gustav to go around and let Johnson in at the back. I heard them exchange some murmured greeting and then the back door was slammed shut. I was still in a state of shock when we got going again and continued to the oil drum yard.

On arrival I saw that everything had changed. There was now a large sign over the double gateway that proclaimed the imminent opening of the car wash. Inside the yard was some newly-installed machinery with numerous attachments. Ted Gresham was sitting in a smart four-door car and when he saw me he got out and came over.

'Glad to see you're nice and punctual,' he said. 'How many men have you got for me?'

'Half a dozen as requested,' I replied. 'There are three in the van plus another three on their way.'

'Excellent.'

Ted went on to inform me that the yard was now equipped with a jet wash and a vacuum cleaner for valeting as well as an extensive selection of soaps, sponges, cloths and polishes. While he was speaking I saw three diminutive men come wandering into the yard. They stood waiting politely near the gate so at an opportune moment I called them across. I also signalled for Gustav and Wolfgang to join us. Johnson was the last to appear. The back door of the van swung open and slowly he stepped out. He took a languid look around the place and scowled before mooching across to hover at the edge of the assembled group.

Ted used his car to demonstrate the correct process for achieving a perfect wash. Valeting was optional, of course. He then took me aside to show me a list of prices for the various treatments.

'Naturally it's cash only,' he said. 'I'll drop by each day just before you close and we can settle the account.'

'Who's going to collect the money from the customers?' I enquired.

'You are.'

'That's not how I understood the agreement,' I said. 'I thought I was merely supplying your labour.'

Ted was plainly disappointed. He puffed out his cheeks and peered around the yard.

'Sorry,' he said at length. 'I suppose I should have made it a little clearer. I wanted you to supply the labour and operate the plant. It needs someone trustworthy in charge.'

The thought occurred to me that handling all the money would give me a much better footing in the business than if I was just a middle man. I glanced at the list of prices and did a quick calculation in my head.

'Alright,' I said. 'Sounds reasonable. I'll run the place for you.'

Ted handed me the keys to the office in the far corner. He then went to his car and opened the boot. Inside were several sets of overalls: all were pale blue with a silver streak.

'I'd like everyone to wear the same colours,' he said. 'It makes them look more like a genuine team.'

Also in the boot was a portable sign that said CAR WASH NOW OPEN. He told me he'd had it made especially.

'Put it out in the road tomorrow,' he said, 'and it should help to pull in a few customers.'

We housed the sign temporarily in the office along with the supply of soap and polish. He then announced that he had other matters to attend to and would therefore leave me to it.

Once he'd gone I distributed the overalls amongst the nascent workforce and then introductions were made. It transpired that the diminutive men were called Joseph, Matthew and Thomas. They were all very unassuming and I sensed they would be reliable workers. Their overalls were rather too big but they promised to alter them overnight to fit better. I had no idea how they were travelling or where they lived. The trio were markedly self-contained, however, and could clearly look after themselves.

'Okay,' I said. 'See you here tomorrow morning at eight.'

Gustav and Wolfgang were busy practising with the jet wash so I walked over to speak to Johnson. He'd remained aloof during the introductions and was now standing gazing at his new overalls.

'Fit you alright?' I asked.

'More or less,' he answered. 'I've only just got accustomed to yellow and green and now I'm in pale blue with a silver streak.'

'What work were you doing?'

'Tyre fitting.'

'But I presume you gave that up.'

'Yes,' he said. 'The company was obviously exploiting me.'

'Seems to be a national trait.'

'They've got all these other fellows from the north who are quite prepared to put up with exploitation.'

'Not you though?'

'No.'

Privately I debated how long Johnson would last at the car wash. He certainly didn't strike me as a very enthusiastic employee. A short distance away Gustav and Wolfgang were still putting the jet wash through its paces while Johnson showed absolutely no interest. More to the point I wondered how he'd managed to win Eva's affections in such a short time. He didn't have any visible charms and I was at a loss to understand what she saw in him.

'I've promised Gustav and Wolfgang I'll buy their breakfast,' I said. 'Do you want to come along too?'

'I'd rather have the money you owe me,' Johnson replied.

'For the night in the factory?'

'Yes.'

'Well, I haven't been paid in full for that yet,' I said. 'It'll just have to be breakfast for the time being: take it or leave it.'

Once I was satisfied that the car wash was ready for the official opening I locked the yard and we prepared to set off towards the cafe. There was then a bit of a disagreement about who should sit in the front of the van. Johnson argued that he deserved preference because he'd known me longer than Gustav and Wolfgang but they countered this by pointing out how many oil drums they'd processed. It transpired that Gustav had been keeping a tally.

'Surely that gives us priority,' he said.

I was tempted to order all three of them into the back but finally I resolved the problem by tossing a coin. The result gave Gustav and Johnson the front seats. The two of them sat side-by-side and brooded sullenly for the entire journey. Wolfgang, meanwhile, perched behind us on a wheel arch.

When we arrived at the cafe I half-expected to see Kevin and Pete's van parked outside. There was no sign of it or them, however, so we went in and I directed Johnson, Gustav and Wolfgang to sit at the eggs, chips and beans table. I then placed an order at the counter before joining them.

'I've been having a think,' I announced, 'and I've decided we'll need to specialise when we get the operation started. Joseph, Matthew and Thomas are all on the small side so they'll be perfectly suited to go inside the cars and do the valeting. Gustav and Wolfgang will be in charge of the jet wash.'

'What about me?' Johnson enquired.

'You'll be polishing windscreens, headlights and hub caps.'

He gazed at me for a few seconds but said nothing.

Eva was on duty and a short while later she presented us with our eggs, chips and beans as well as bread and butter and a mug of tea apiece. I'd realised it would help to ease tensions a little if I shared the same meal as the others rather than sitting at a separate table with a cheese and tomato omelette. Fortunately there was less rancour directed at me than between Johnson and Gustav. Already I could detect a rivalry developing: there had even been a slight tussle about who sat where at the table. They simply did not get on together which was odd because actually they had quite a lot in common. Both were highly contemptuous of the native population and held strong views about their customs and practises. They tended to voice these opinions openly and I suspected that if they ever joined forces they could cause difficulties (doubly so if they thought they were being exploited). For my part I was determined this should never happen. The solution was simple: I would devise a system of payment that favoured those workers who were most productive. This, I was certain, would nourish the rivalry between Johnson and Gustav and prevent them from ever becoming a threat to my authority.

I was pleased to see that Eva retained a professional manner when dealing with Johnson. Whenever she came to our table she treated him as coolly as the rest of us: he received no more than a passing nod from her and nobody would guess that they lived together in the flat upstairs. Even so I still found the situation most uncomfortable, especially when ultimately we departed the cafe and left Johnson behind.

'I'll pick you up at seven thirty tomorrow morning,' I said, before going to the counter and paying for the four breakfasts.

When we got outside Wolfgang started asking questions about Johnson and Eva which I refused to answer. Instead, I reached into my pocket and produced a wad of money. I now had enough confidence in our future earnings to pay Gustav and Wolfgang some more of the wages I owed them. We then climbed into the van and headed for the general store so that we could replenish our provisions. After we'd all stocked up we were about to resume our journey to the fairground when a thought occurred to me.

'We've got a free afternoon ahead of us,' I said. 'Why don't we go and open the car wash immediately?'

They both jumped at the opportunity so I swiftly spun the van around and set off in the opposite direction. On arrival at the yard we unlocked the double gates and swung them wide open. I retrieved Ted Gresham's sign from the office and instructed Wolfgang to put it in a prominent position outside the gates. Gustav started getting the equipment ready while I gave the office a bit of a tidy up. It was only small and had clearly been out of use for quite some time. There was a desk and a chair, however, and once I'd given the window a clean the place began to look functional again. In the desk drawer I found an empty ledger which I decided to use for recording the daily takings. After that it was simply a matter of waiting for our first customer.

In the event it was only about twenty minutes later that a car pulled cautiously into the yard. The driver wound down his window. I walked over and asked him which service he required.

'Full wash and valet please,' he replied. 'I'm glad I spotted you. I haven't had a chance to clean it for weeks.'

'Alright, sir,' I said, 'if you'd just like to wait over there we'll have it done for you in a jiffy.'

I think we all surprised ourselves by the efficiency with which we carried out our work. Gustav appeared especially adept with the jet wash and the car was soon ready for the next stage in the process. Wolfgang carefully vacuumed the interior and then all three of us busied ourselves applying the finishing touches. By the time we'd returned the keys to their owner the vehicle was absolutely sparkling clean.

For the second car of the afternoon I took a turn operating the vacuum myself. I soon found out that I wasn't much suited to this particular task. It involved getting into all sorts of cramped positions and only served to confirm my idea of deploying Joseph, Matthew and Thomas in the role. For the time being, though, l left Wolfgang in charge of vacuum cleaning while Gustav handled the jet wash.

Another lesson I learnt fairly quickly was that if I made an admiring remark about somebody's car they generally added a generous tip to the basic price. It was patently clear that the cleanliness of a car contributed markedly to individual happiness and I speculated that the same principle might hold true on a national scale. I then began to develop the idea of adapting the office into a sort of waiting room so that customers wouldn't need to hang around the yard while their cars were being seen to. Even better, we could perhaps provide complimentary coffee and pastries! As the hours passed and the cars came and went I began to feel that our prospects for success were improving rapidly.

I was just pondering whether to treat Gustav and Wolfgang to some fish and chips when I noticed another car arriving. For some reason, however, it didn't enter the yard but instead parked opposite the gates. After a while a man got out and walked over. He was carrying a clipboard and had a rather official look about him.

'I'm afraid I must request you to suspend operations at once,' he said. 'You're violating the terms of the lease.'

'I think you'll find,' I replied, 'that the lease has been taken over by a Mr Gresham.'

The man gave me a prolonged look.

'Yes, I know all about the lease,' he said firmly, 'but you weren't supposed to begin commercial operations until tomorrow.'

'Oh, sorry,' I said. 'I didn't realise. Is it okay to finish the car we're doing at the moment? We're about halfway through.'

'No,' he said. 'You have to cease now.'

The car in question had been driven into the yard by our first woman customer. It was a shiny red model that hardly needed cleaning but nonetheless was currently smothered with soap. I was now obliged to tell her that we couldn't complete the job. Needless to say she was highly displeased. She told me it was the last time she would visit such a slipshod outfit and she assured me I wouldn't be seeing her again. The man with the clip board continued watching our activities and didn't depart until he was satisfied that we had fully shut down the car wash. I brought the sign in from the road and put it in the office.

All this interference was slightly annoying because I'd already begun entering the day's takings in the ledger. I fleetingly considered tearing out the offending page but then decided to leave it just as it was. If we all kept quiet Ted Gresham need never know about the official visit and hopefully he would welcome the additional earnings we'd accrued.

As it happened I didn't see Ted for almost a week. He'd initially told me that he would drop by daily at the close of business but I soon discovered that he was a very busy man with little time to spare. In consequence I was able fully to take charge of running the car wash. A fixed routine swiftly developed. Each morning I woke

Gustav and Wolfgang early and we headed to the cafe to pick up Johnson and have a brief pause for breakfast. On arrival at the yard we'd inevitably find Joseph, Matthew and Thomas already waiting outside the gates. As soon as the first customer arrived we'd all swing into action with everyone specialising in the roles I'd allocated. There was no safe place in the office to deposit the cash we collected so I locked it in the van's glove compartment. At lunchtime I'd go and collect fish and chips and then we'd continue to plough on until dusk.

As I'd predicted, Joseph, Matthew and Thomas were the best suited to valeting. They climbed in and out of the constricted spaces with ease and always left the interiors looking spick-and-span. I soon noticed that they all had religious symbols hanging from chains around their necks. During quiet periods they assembled in an unused corner of the yard and I assumed they'd gone there to pray. This didn't worry me at all because when they weren't praying they were very hard working.

By now I'd decided to pay everyone an equal daily wage supplemented with a variable productivity bonus which I would calculate at the end of the week. The daily payment was naturally subject to certain administrative deductions but it meant that each evening the workforce departed with at least some money in their pockets. Wolfgang had made it clear that he was happy to ride in the back of the van if it would prevent quarrelling between Johnson and Gustav. After Johnson had been dropped off Wolfgang would join us in the front and we'd return to the fairground.

The three of us were becoming quite accustomed to living together in the brick hut though plainly the situation couldn't last forever. The nights were becoming longer and colder and Gustav spent more and more time attending to the cast iron stove. He was forever fiddling with the vent to try and make it burn better. Sometimes he fiddled with it so much that the fire went out entirely. Meanwhile he kept sending Wolfgang in search of yet more sticks. Fortunately I wasn't around to witness many of these goings on. I had no intention of passing each evening with Gustav and Wolfgang when the lights of The Wheatsheaf beckoned.

Initially I considered inviting Johnson to accompany me but I soon realised the idea had many drawbacks. I wasn't even sure if I liked him very much. I'd been vaguely acquainted with him before we embarked on our trip to these shores yet I would hardly have called him a friend. As a matter of fact now that we were working together he was proving to be a bit of a nuisance. For a start he didn't have his own transport so I was constantly having to pick him up and drop him off. This became an increasing source of irritation as the days passed (especially since Joseph, Matthew and Thomas managed to get to the yard perfectly well unaided). Admittedly Johnson performed his allotted tasks at the car wash adequately enough. At the same time, though, he always gave the impression that he deemed his talents to be undervalued. Hence he was never satisfied with the money I gave him. Then there was his undisguised hostility towards the locals. He'd arrived in this country to try and help cure its people of their sorrows but now it seemed his good intentions had gone by the board. There really was no telling how he would behave in a public house. Finally, of course, I still found it infuriating that Johnson had won Eva's favour so easily.

For these reasons I decided to go to the pub alone. On some occasions I walked and on others I took the van, depending on circumstances.

One evening I sat through an entire quiz unable to answer any of the questions. Frank and his team won (as usual) and afterwards I sat reflecting on how little I understood of this country and its inhabitants. To judge by what I heard during the quiz their prime interests were sport, television and pop music with only sporadic forays into other branches of learning. Mathematics, science and engineering were apparently not considered interesting enough to be included. Chivalric words and deeds, by contrast, had a strong showing: who said what to whom on the eve of battle, in the middle of the Antarctic, in the depths of the jungle, in the heat of the desert or when his ship went to the bottom of the sea. There were never any questions about foreign history, foreign explorers or foreign affairs (although I suspected Frank's team would have been able to answer them if required). The only exception were foreign footballers whose goals were frequently referenced in tie-break questions. Vaguely I tried to imagine similar quizzes taking place in faraway lands but in the end I gave up. They could only happen in this country.

I was still lost in thought when Eva came and sat down beside me with a large glass of wine in her hand. She'd been collecting empties as usual and was now on her break. We engaged in a little small talk about the quiz (Eva didn't know any of the answers either) and I told her my plans for improving customer facilities at the car wash. She listened with interest but once again I got the feeling she was working towards something. We lapsed into silence for a few moments and then finally she turned to face me.

'Do you know what I would wish for,' she asked, 'if I could have a wish?'

'No,' I replied.

'I'd wish that Johnson could be more like you.'

It goes without saying that I was lost for words. Clearly Eva saw qualities in me that I was unaware of and I sat there trying hard to think what they might be. As I saw it the list was quite short. I was now in charge of a burgeoning car wash facility (and actually in possession of a significant quantity of cash) but I sensed she was looking a little deeper than that.

'You mean because I've got my own transport and he hasn't?'

'Not really, no,' she said, 'but obviously it would help.'

'Generosity to others?'

'No.'

'What then?'

'Eva!'

The voice belonged to Norman. He was calling her from behind the bar.

'Yes?'

'Sorry to trouble you when you're on your break but I've got a beer barrel running out. Can you take over here while I go downstairs?'

'Okay.'

Eva gave me a smile before finishing her wine and rising to her feet.

'We'll talk about it another time,' she said.

'Alright.'

I hoped that maybe she planned to resume the conversation later in the evening but in fact it wasn't to be. Once she was ensconced behind the bar there suddenly seemed to be more customers going up to buy drinks. When

Norman returned from the cellar he decided to retain her on serving duties for the time being and went around collecting the empty glasses himself. Briefly I considered volunteering to help him but in truth I knew the gesture would be futile. Soon afterwards last orders were called which meant there'd be no hope of getting to speak to Eva for at least another twenty minutes. By then the pub would be emptying and the opportunity lost.

Next morning when we arrived at the cafe Johnson informed me that Eva had changed shifts with a colleague and had already set off to do a day's work as a traffic warden. Obviously I said nothing to him about her enigmatic remark of the previous evening (especially as Gustav and Wolfgang were both present and eavesdropping intently). After breakfast we proceeded to the car wash to resume our daily labours. Joseph, Matthew and Thomas were already there and we swiftly got the operation running. I took it upon myself to greet newly-arrived customers and after they'd gone I recorded each transaction in the ledger. By now I'd discovered that the office window was handy for keeping an eye on my fellow workers. This was imperative because

Johnson and Gustav were still rather prickly with each another: on one occasion Johnson took over the jet wash when a new vehicle arrived and insisted he could do a better job. Gustav protested to me about this but actually I could see no harm in a bit of healthy competition between them. Consequently I decided to rotate the exterior tasks so that Johnson, Gustav and Wolfgang took turns with the jet washing, the wiping of windscreens and the polishing of hub caps and headlights.

The valeting, however, remained exclusively the domain of Joseph, Matthew and Thomas. The three of them were evidently very closely bonded and had devised a system of working that needed no improvement. They mostly kept themselves to themselves but were never unfriendly or standoffish. After a while I noticed that they'd decorated their corner of the yard with numerous religious artefacts. I wasn't certain of the precise purpose of these but if they served to keep them happy it was fine by me.

A further three days passed before Ted Gresham eventually made an appearance. It was late afternoon and we were just preparing to close when his car pulled in through the gates. He parked in the corner by the office and I went out to speak to him.

'Looks as if you've got it all running nicely,' he commented.

'Yes, I'm fairly pleased,' I said, 'and of course I've got some money for you.'

I unlocked the van and removed the cash from the glove compartment. Ted counted it and then handed me my agreed percentage.

'I'll try to come by a bit more regularly,' he said, 'but I've been extremely busy just lately.'

'Well, I'll expect you when I see you,' I replied. 'By the way if you want to check the figures they're all recorded in the ledger.'

'No, no,' he answered. 'That's alright. I'm sure I can trust you.'

We watched as the team put yet another vehicle through the cleaning process.

'Do you want us to do yours quickly before we close?' I suggested.

'Ah, that's very kind of you,' said Ted. 'Thank you.'

I made sure his car received a very thorough service but afterwards I was slightly disappointed when he didn't offer to pay. Evidently he believed that as proprietor he was entitled to a free wash. I knew this could cause a potential future complication because Gustav was keeping a separate record of how many cars we dealt with each day. After Ted had departed I saw Gustav speaking quietly to Wolfgang and then he approached me.

'When do we receive our productivity bonus?' he enquired.

'At the end of the week,' I said. 'When I've done the calculation.'

'And what about the boss's car?'

'I'll take account of that.'

Seemingly Johnson overheard the discussion because he now joined in.

'That man's obviously exploiting us,' he said. 'We should throw him out and run the car wash ourselves.'

'We can't just take it over,' I replied. 'Ted Gresham's the leaseholder.'

'Pah!' said Johnson. 'The laws in this country are so archaic. Everybody bows and scrapes to these property men.'

'Maybe so,' I said, 'but I'm afraid that's the way it is.'

'And you're one of his minions.'

Johnson appeared to have forgotten that I'd done him a favour by finding him a job. I'd done it solely to please Eva and really I'd received nothing tangible in return. For this reason I resolved to take Johnson down a peg or two.

'I think you might have to start coming to work under your own steam,' I said. 'I can't just go on picking you up every morning.'

'But you stop at the cafe anyway,' he countered, 'to have your breakfast.'

'Maybe so,' I said, 'but I can't guarantee it.'

There was a petulant silence in the van when we drove home that evening. The lights of the cafe (and the flat above) looked bright and inviting when we dropped Johnson off and I concluded that really he had nothing to complain about. Gustav and Wolfgang murmured something to one another and then we headed back to the fairground. I was now heartily tired of being in their company twenty four hours a day and so later I again sought refuge in The Wheatsheaf.

Immediately I laid eyes on Eva I detected a change in her demeanour. She was now stationed permanently behind the bar and was markedly cool with me when she handed me my pint. I could only assume that Johnson had been grousing to her. I tried the usual small talk but it got me nowhere so I went and sat at the corner table feeling more than a little regretful.

The only consolation came when a woman emerged from the saloon bar and began collecting glasses. It was Tamara and she recognised me at once. She paused a moment at my table.

'Job number three?' I enquired

'Yes,' she replied. 'Just a couple of nights a week for the present while they try me out.'

'You'll probably be alright.'

'Did you hear what happened at the protest camp?'

'No.'

'They've been served with a notice of eviction,' she said. 'Twenty eight days to disperse.'

'What did Harcourt have to say about that?'

'Oh, he took it all in his stride as usual.'

I thought I saw Tamara's eyes sparkle when she spoke of Harcourt. Next instant a sharp word from Eva reminded her that she was here to collect glasses not gossip with the customers. A little later when it was time for her break it never occurred to her to come and sit beside me. Instead, she retreated into the saloon bar and I didn't see her again that evening.

13

One afternoon the car wash was in full swing when we had a visit from Bob Twigg. He parked his flatbed lorry opposite the double gates and then walked across to see me. I noticed as he approached that he was moving rather stiffly.

'Hello Bob,' I said. 'Everything okay?'

'No,' he replied. 'I've gone and done my back in.'

'Sorry to hear that.'

'Quite inconvenient really because I've just picked up a nice bit of business.'

'Have you sorted out some new premises then?'

'No, not yet. This is a sort of in-between job.'

He peered across the yard towards where Joseph, Matthew and Thomas were hard at work.

'I don't suppose you could spare me one of those three for a couple of hours?' he asked. 'There's a bit of heavy lifting to do and I don't think I'll manage on my own.'

'No, sorry,' I said. 'We've got quite a few cars coming through at present and this is generally our busiest time of day.'

'What about the other three?'

'No, sorry again but they're all in specialised roles.'

Bob gave a resigned sigh.

'Thought as much,' he said. 'Oh well, it was worth a try.'

I pondered for a few seconds.

'Tell you what,' I said, 'I'll come with you if you like. It'll make a change and I'm sure I can leave this lot unsupervised for a while.'

Obviously I had to delegate responsibility so after a moment's deliberation I selected Joseph to take care of the money. I took him aside and told him to enter all transactions in the ledger. Cash was to be locked in the van's glove compartment. I then informed the others that Joseph was temporarily in charge. Matthew and Thomas readily acquiesced but Johnson, Gustav and Wolfgang all looked far from happy with my decision. Evidently they considered themselves somehow superior to their workmates in the valeting department and I realised the team wasn't quite as close knit as I'd hitherto believed.

Well as far as I was concerned that was their problem not mine. I joined Bob in his lorry and we soon got going.

It swiftly transpired that we weren't heading for any single destination but rather a number of locations dotted around a large area. Bob had found out that there was a thriving market for second-hand pallets and he'd been on the telephone all morning tracking down a few. He wanted me to help him load them onto the lorry. I rather enjoyed riding along roads I'd never travelled before. We called at a variety of places including warehouses, factory premises and a bakery. At each stop we picked up a dozen or so pallets from people who were seemingly glad to get rid of them.

'They take up a lot of space,' said Bob, 'so we're actually doing them a favour.'

Unfortunately there weren't enough pallets to make up a full load. After the final call some unused space remained at the rear of the lorry and I could see Bob was cross with himself for his apparent miscalculation.

'I know where there are a few more pallets,' I said, 'if you don't mind driving a bit further.'

I told him about the stack of pallets at the fairground and he seized the chance at once. We arrived there about half an hour later and I was pleased to see that my padlock was still in place on the galvanised chain. I jumped down from the lorry and removed it temporarily.

'This your piece of land, is it?' Bob enquired, as we proceeded down the concrete road.

'Well,' I said, 'I'm just looking after it really.'

There were ten pallets stacked over by the electricity pylon: just sufficient to complete the load. Before we departed I showed Bob the brick hut.

'Three of us are staying in here at present,' I said, 'but actually there's room for three more.'

Bob was clearly impressed. I opened the door and he studied the interior with interest.

'This would be just perfect,' he announced at length.

'What for?'

He went on to explain that Joseph, Matthew and Thomas were currently living in a caravan in his garden. His wife had been complaining about their presence for weeks but he hadn't had the heart to ask them to move out. The brick hut offered the ideal solution to his problem.

'Naturally it would have to be with your agreement,' he said, 'but I can assure you they're very clean and tidy.'

'Do you charge them rent for the caravan?' I enquired.

'Indirectly,' he said. 'I deduct it from their wages.'

'But they're not working for you at the moment.'

'No,' he said, 'so there's nothing to deduct.'

By the time we got back to the car wash I'd decided that, yes, I would accommodate Joseph, Matthew and Thomas in the brick hut. Bob dropped me off outside the gates and gave me some cash for my trouble before driving away. I entered the yard and saw the entire team hard at work finishing off a gleaming car.

Well, almost the entire team.

Actually there were only five of them. I glanced towards the office and saw Gustav sitting at the desk perusing the ledger. He was so engrossed that he didn't notice me approaching.

'Excuse me, Gustav,' I said. 'What do you think you're doing?'

'I'm just trying to calculate how much you owe me and Wolfgang,' he replied, 'to save you doing it.'

He showed not a flicker of remorse at having been caught in the act. He merely remained sitting at the desk as though he was perfectly entitled to be there. I picked up the ledger and leafed through the pages.

'Whose handwriting is this?' I asked.

'Joseph's,' said Gustav, 'but I've taken over because he was obviously struggling with the figures.'

'Really?'

I examined the entries made by Joseph. They were concise and legible and gave no indication that he was having any difficulty at all. Nevertheless Gustav had thought fit to usurp his position.

Just then Johnson appeared in the doorway.

'You should put me in charge,' he announced, 'not Gustav.'

'Neither of you are in charge,' I replied. 'Joseph is entirely capable of running the place if I happen to be absent.'

'But he and his pals keep stopping to pray in that sacred corner of theirs.'

'Only during the lulls.'

'No, it's all the time!'.

'He's right,' said Gustav.

I peered through the window. Across the yard Joseph, Matthew and Thomas were beavering away inside yet another car while Wolfgang busily polished the hub cabs. On the surface all was well but plainly Johnson and Gustav saw it from a different perspective. Whether they would suspend their rivalry over the matter was hard to predict so I moved swiftly to prevent the risk of further escalation.

'Look, I'll tell you what I'll do,' I said. 'I'll keep an eye on those three for the next few days and I'll check how often they stop and pray.'

'Okay,' said Gustav.

'And in the meantime you can keep your nose out of the ledger.'

Johnson remained standing in the doorway while Gustav squeezed past him and returned to work. I placed the ledger in the drawer of the desk and when I looked up Johnson was still there.

'Yes?' I asked. 'Was there something else?'

'I was just wondering,' he said. 'Will we be getting our productivity bonus tomorrow?'

'Correct,' I said, 'after lunch.'

'That's good. I'm desperate for some cash.'

'What about your daily payment?'

'It's already gone.'

'How come?'

'Eva's started charging me rent for the flat.'

All of a sudden Johnson didn't appear so full of himself. He stood in the doorway looking a little deflated and for a moment I was almost sorry for him. Inside, though, I felt a surge of elation. Clearly Eva was not quite as smitten with Johnson as I'd supposed. Perhaps I'd misinterpreted the frosty treatment she'd given me the other night: perhaps she was simply steeling herself to deal with the question of rent.

'Well,' I remarked, 'she certainly seems rather astute when it comes to money matters.'

'I'll say she is,' Johnson affirmed. 'She's already got a bank account, a national insurance number and a tax code.'

'But you haven't?'

'No.'

Bearing in mind that Johnson was my only proper link with Eva I decided to treat him with some sympathy.

'Actually,' I said, producing some notes from my pocket, 'I'm now in a position to pay you for the night in the factory.'

This was intended as a friendly gesture but for some reason Johnson regarded it with mistrust.

'So why couldn't you pay me before?' he demanded.

'Because I needed cash to put fuel in the van and buy all the breakfasts amongst other things.'

'Oh,' said Johnson, 'yes I suppose you did.'

He grudgingly took the money I proffered before strolling out of the office. The transaction was witnessed by Gustav and Wolfgang and a couple of minutes later they appeared at the door.

'Are you paying our bonus today?' Gustav enquired.

'No,' I said. 'Tomorrow.'

'But we've just seen you paying Johnson.'

'That was for unrelated work. Nothing to do with the car wash.'

The pair of them wandered back outside and across the empty yard. There were no customers at present and I began thinking of winding up for the day. First, though, I had another matter to deal with. I emerged from the office and walked with a purposeful stride towards the corner where Joseph, Matthew and Thomas had gathered as usual. Johnson, Gustav and Wolfgang watched me go. Hopefully they would assume I intended to raise the subject of praying but actually I was on my way to discuss the provision of accommodation. Such was the multifaceted role of a competent manager. As I drew near I saw that the three valets were indeed praying. They were all facing in the same direction so I hovered close by until Joseph happened to notice me. At a signal from him they all stopped praying at once.

'Sorry to interrupt,' I said, 'but I wanted to have a word with all of you.'

'It's perfectly alright, sir,' said Joseph. 'We can pause at any time.'

'By the way there's no need to call me 'sir'.'

He gave me an obedient nod and I then went on to tell the three of them about the brick hut. They welcomed the offer with gratitude. Apparently they'd been fully aware of Bob Twigg's wife's hostility towards them and had been anxious to find an alternative to the caravan for quite a while.

'Mr Twigg's garden is very nice,' Joseph added, presumably to show that there were no hard feelings, 'and so is his wife.'

I explained that there would be a small rental charge deducted from their wages and this, too, they accepted. We agreed they would all move into the brick hut the following day. I decided to postpone informing Gustav and Wolfgang about the new arrangements until a more suitable opportunity arose.

I was about to lock the double gates when a car came charging up the road. At first I thought it was a late customer but in fact it was Ted Gresham. When he screeched to a halt, got out and slammed the door I sensed he was in a bad mood. In his hand he was clutching a document.

'Are you trying to put me out of business?' he snapped.

'No, of course not,' I replied.

'Well, had do you explain this?'

He thrust the document into my hand and I read the contents. It was a letter to Ted from the property company that owned the yard. Seemingly the terms of the lease had been violated and the lease was therefore suspended under Clause 7.5 (b). (The suspension could be overridden at any time on payment of a penalty charge.)

'You opened the car wash a day earlier than we agreed,' Ted uttered. 'Were you operating behind my back?'

'No, sorry,' I said. 'It was a mistake.'

'A likely story.'

'No really. I can prove it. All transactions were recorded in the ledger.'

I led him to the office and showed him the entries for the first day. He compared them to his own record of the money I'd given him and they matched exactly. I was exonerated from operating behind his back but even so he was still vexed about the penalty charge.

'I'm afraid I'll have to deduct it from your percentage,' he announced. 'Shame actually. You've got the place running nicely.'

I wasn't sure how much of a cloud this put me under in Ted Gresham's opinion. All I knew for certain was that the deduction would wipe out my earnings for the entire week. Once I'd paid everyone their productivity bonus I would be left with barely two coins to rub together. Reluctantly I went to the van and removed a large wad of notes from the glove compartment. I gave Ted a sizeable proportion.

'Right,' he said. 'I'll pay the penalty charge directly.'

'Okay.'

'Do you want a receipt?'

'No,' I said. 'I trust you.'

'You should be able to open as normal tomorrow morning.'

He made it clear that he didn't want any more shenanigans (as he put it) and I knew I was going to have to watch my step in my further dealings with him. After he'd gone I climbed into the van and sat behind the wheel. There was no doubt that the exchange between Ted Gresham and me had been observed by Johnson, Gustav and Wolfgang and in consequence I felt somewhat diminished. I half-expected Johnson to repeat his assertion that we should throw Ted out of the yard and run the car wash ourselves but in the event he said nothing. As a matter of fact the three of them remained silent all the way to the cafe. I assumed they sensed I wouldn't be in the mood for small talk. When we dropped Johnson off, however, he surprised me by suggesting that all four of us should go to the pub together later. It transpired that the idea had first been mooted by Gustav while they were waiting for me to return to the van.

'Okay,' I said, 'just as long as everybody pays for their own drinks.'

It was arranged that we would collect Johnson again in two hours time and then we headed back to the fairground. Having resolved the perceived problem of Joseph, Matthew and Thomas I was fairly optimistic that industrial relations were perhaps moving onto a sounder footing. The only problem was that out of all of us I was temporarily the poorest.

I had no idea whether Johnson had ever been to The Wheatsheaf (or any pub for that matter). There was a chance he'd accompanied Eva there at some time but if so he made no mention of it to me. Wolfgang had a single prior visit to his credit and Gustav none at all, so it was with slight trepidation that I led the three of them into the public bar later that evening. Eva was on duty behind the counter and I hoped her presence would guarantee they'd all be on their best behaviour. She greeted us professionally and took my order for a pint of my usual. Johnson, Gustav and Wolfgang all placed the same order before following me to the only empty table. We were lucky to get hold of it. As soon as we'd walked in I'd realised this was the night of the quiz and now the pub was filling up rapidly. Briefly I considered entering ourselves as a team but I soon dismissed the notion: we wouldn't stand a chance against the likes of Frank and his pals.

Once the quizmaster had begun distributing the answer sheets, however, both Johnson and Gustav expressed a desire to join in. It then occurred to me that taking part in a quiz might help them in the process of integration. I made enquiries and discovered that the entry fee was a shilling per team. We decided to pool our resources and a few minutes later we'd successfully enrolled.

My three companions were plainly astonished by the reverential hush that descended on the public bar when the quiz began. The only sound was the voice of the quizmaster (Jerry again: he conducted the ceremony every week apparently) augmented by the scratching of pencils and occasional whispers between team members. Gustav initially had trouble adapting to the enforced silence. He'd been led to believe that pubs in this country were full of rowdy drunkards ready to pick a fight if somebody looked at them the wrong way. Instead, he was surrounded by legions of studious individuals who kept 'shushing' him if he spoke too loudly. As for the questions themselves he clearly found most of them completely bewildering. When he was unable to answer he gave a long drawn-out sigh of resignation which triggered further demands to 'shush'. Johnson, in the meantime, had taken charge of the pencil and paper. He happened to know the answer to a single question (concerning the colours of a particular national flag) and this made him believe he should therefore be elevated to team captain. At one point during the quiz I caught sight of Eva. She was observing events from behind the bar and seemed to be taking a quiet delight in Johnson's evident struggle. Ultimately I contributed three correct answers while Johnson, Gustav and Wolfgang managed two between them. The winning score was twenty nine (Frank's team) and was greeted with a hearty cheer from the pub's entire clientele.

'Obviously a primitive ritual designed to fortify social distinctions,' remarked Johnson.

Gustav was even more disdainful. He said we might as well have spent the evening in a monastery rather than this 'glorified examination hall'. Actually the silence had now transformed into a hubbub of bonhomie but Gustav patently failed to appreciate the difference.

'So you won't be coming again?' I enquired.

'Not likely,' he said.

He examined his glass of beer.

'Two thirds of this comprises excise duty,' he continued. 'The other third is practically undrinkable.'

'A waste of hard-earned money,' added Wolfgang.

I was rather gratified by their verdict if it meant the pair of them wouldn't be joining me in the pub anymore. Johnson, though, took an altogether broader outlook. He may have come bottom in the quiz but he viewed this as a challenge rather than a defeat. Moreover he actually liked the beer on offer. He made frequent return visits to the bar and I soon began to wonder how long his funds would last. If they ran out prematurely he'd be unable to meet Eva's demand for rent. This in turn would be a test of her tolerance. I awaited the outcome with interest.

14

Next morning Joseph, Matthew and Thomas arrived at the car wash each carrying a hold-all. Seemingly these contained all their possessions.

They also presented me with a flower.

'Taken from the garden with permission from Mrs Twigg,' said Joseph, 'and her blessing.'

I suggested that they put their baggage directly into the back of the van. Gustav and Wolfgang monitored these proceedings with suspicion but I offered them no explanation and set everyone to work cleaning the first car of the day. As promised, however, I kept a watchful eye on Joseph, Matthew and Thomas to make sure they weren't taking too many liberties. As the hours passed I reached the conclusion that the breaks they took were no longer than anybody else's. They merely put them to a different use.

Johnson had looked a little worse for wear when I'd picked him up outside the cafe at seven thirty and I speculated that he'd been obliged to sleep on the sofa. Not that my personal situation was very much better. Breakfast at the cafe had used up most of my remaining money and when lunchtime came I was obliged to suspend my usual practise of buying everyone's fish and chips and deducting the cost from their wages. Joseph, Matthew and Thomas had never partaken anyway (I assumed they were fasting) and now the others were excluded too. I paid them their daily allowance out of the morning's takings and explained that henceforth it would have to be cash in advance for their fish and chips.

'Plaice or cod?' I enquired when I took their individual orders.

They all chose cod, which simplified matters a great deal.

Fortunately business was thriving and by late afternoon I'd accumulated a new supply of cash. All was satisfactory when Ted Gresham called in for his share. He made no mention of the lease so I guessed it was all settled. After he'd gone I studied the ledger and carefully worked out the week's productivity bonus.

I now had to face a matter that I'd been postponing all day long: it was only fair to inform Gustav and Wolfgang that there would be three new tenants joining us in the brick hut. Generally when I paid out the bonuses I simply walked around the yard casually handing them over to the individuals concerned. Today, for a change, I called them one by one into the office. Wolfgang was first. When I told him the news he replied that he and Gustav had suspected as much when they saw the three hold-alls. I asked if he had any objection and he said he would have to consult with Gustav. Johnson was next and his main concern was the size of his bonus.

'You'll be pleased to learn,' I told him, 'that productivity is up on last week.'

'That means even more money for your friend Gresham,' he retorted.

'He's not my friend,' I said. 'He's a business associate.'

Naturally I had no complaints from either Joseph or Matthew when they received their bonuses. They both called me 'sir' and thanked me profusely. Gustav was fourth in line. I knew that Wolfgang would already have apprised him of the accommodation plan so when he walked into the office I braced myself for a verbal assault. Instead, he coolly notified me that if I went ahead with the new living arrangements then he and Wolfgang would quit working at the car wash.

'You won't find anyone as productive as us,' he announced. 'People in this country don't want to work.'

I thanked him for letting me know and handed him his bonus. The final visit came from Thomas. He was polite, affable, gentle and hard-working just like his two compatriots and frankly I couldn't see why Gustav and Wolfgang were so up in arms against all of them.

Nonetheless the episode had left me in a quandary. I couldn't really afford to lose Gustav and Wolfgang now that the car wash was running so smoothly but at the same time I was reluctant to let down Joseph, Matthew and Thomas. There was a chance, of course, that Gustav had been bluffing. If so, he was taking a substantial risk. We both knew that if I called his bluff then he and Wolfgang would end up homeless and jobless. In view of this I decided to carry on as normal and see what happened.

The van was fully-laden when we departed the yard that evening after I'd locked up. Johnson and Gustav took their usual places in the front seats while Wolfgang, Joseph, Matthew and Thomas all crowded into the back. By now Johnson had learnt that six of us would be sharing the brick hut and as soon as we got going he began stirring things up by mentioning that he was thinking of having sardines for supper. I told him to please be quiet or he might have to walk to work tomorrow. This did the trick and for the rest of the journey he was silent. In due course we dropped Johnson off, then Wolfgang moved into the front seat and we continued to the fairground.

On arrival I pulled up in front of the galvanised chain and asked Wolfgang to get out and unfasten the padlock. He returned a moment later and said that the key didn't fit. I went and had a look for myself and discovered that during the day my padlock had been replaced by a different one. There was a tag attached to it imprinted with the words RAILWAY PROPERTY BOARD. I then remembered Barry Barton telling me that he'd removed countless padlocks in the past and that the railway property board kept fitting new ones. This was plainly the latest in the series. It occurred to me that it would serve the same purpose as my own padlock if it deterred unwanted visitors. The trouble was I now had the inconvenience of having to leave the van parked in the lay-by. Still, there was nothing I could do about it so we all got out and walked down the concrete road to the brick hut. The light was fading as I showed Joseph, Matthew and Thomas into their new home. They were delighted with its abundant roominess (apparently the caravan in Bob Twigg's garden had been fairly small) and immediately began unpacking their hold-alls. Meanwhile Gustav and Wolfgang were busy swapping their bedding around. They'd already seized the bunk beds nearest the cast iron stove. I thought they were making rather a fuss about it all just to prove that they'd been there longer than the three newcomers. I offered Joseph, Matthew and Thomas a choice of the other bunks and then I gracefully took the remaining place for myself.

Needless to say the first evening the six of us spent together in the brick hut wasn't entirely plain sailing. Once they'd picked their bunks Joseph, Matthew and Thomas then went out into the fairground in search of somewhere to pray. They didn't appear again until after dark by which time the rest of us had finished our supper. We soon learnt that their dietary requirements were different to ours (it involved long periods of fasting) but they assured us that we needn't worry and it would not affect us in any way. There was further prayer, followed by extensive hand and foot washing at the standpipe. Meanwhile Gustav and Wolfgang emitted unrelenting sighs of discontentment as they lay fidgeting in their bunks.

Despite all this I managed to get a reasonable night's sleep. In the morning I awoke early and saw that Joseph, Matthew and Thomas had already risen. When I went outside I spotted them over by the electricity pylon. They were conducting their prayers in full view of passing trains. When I recalled that I'd prohibited Gustav and Wolfgang from flying their national flag I realised I needed to be similarly firm with the other three. Otherwise we'd simply be drawing too much attention to ourselves. When they'd finished praying I took Joseph aside and asked him if they could possibly find somewhere a little more discreet.

'Of course, sir,' he said. 'We can be very flexible.'

Their flexibility was demonstrated when we stopped for breakfast at seven thirty. They insisted they needed nothing because they'd eaten before dawn and were now fasting. Instead, they waited in the van while I went into the cafe followed by Gustav and Wolfgang. The two of them had said nothing more about 'quitting' the car wash so I directed them to the eggs, chips and beans table and placed an order at the counter. We were soon joined by Johnson. He showed me a newspaper advertisement he'd come across:

NEW GOVERNMENT AGENCY REQUIRES STAFF FOR
SENSITIVE WORK IN PUBLIC DOMAIN
COMPETITIVE RATES PAID
APPLICANTS MUST BE PROFICIENT IN AT LEAST
ONE LANGUAGE

'I quite like the sound of that,' Johnson announced. 'I think I'll apply.'

'So presumably you'll be leaving the car wash?' I asked.

'In due course, yes,' he said, 'but you'll easily find a replacement.'

I glanced at Gustav but he pretended not to hear. When Eva brought our breakfasts she peered at the advertisement and shook her head.

'In this country,' she said, 'the term 'competitive rates' is totally meaningless.'

'I know,' said Johnson, 'but I can always negotiate.'

I had to admit that my admiration for Eva was deepening all the time. Not only was she self-assured and hard working but she also seemed to possess a much surer grasp of the realities of life than all the rest of us put together. Certainly more so than Johnson. He appeared convinced he was in with a chance of landing a job and naturally I said nothing to discourage him. Eva gave me an unreadable look when she handed me my tea and I spent the rest of the day wondering what it meant.

I also wondered how Joseph, Matthew and Thomas managed to work so many hours without eating a morsel. They were easily the most productive members of the team (despite Gustav's claim) yet to my knowledge they'd had nothing since before dawn. After observing them for the entire morning I made a mental note to adjust the next week's bonus in their favour. At lunchtime I went around taking orders for fish and chips. Gustav and Wolfgang then both announced that they were tired of fish and chips and would like to try something different for a change. After a brief discussion it was agreed that I would pay them their daily cash allowance and they would go and choose their own lunches.

'You can have half an hour,' I said, as they wandered out through the gateway, 'so you'd better get a move on.'

A few minutes later I set off in the van to collect some fish and chips for Johnson and myself. When I reached the parade of shops I expected to see Gustav and Wolfgang but actually there was no sign of them. The usual delay occurred while my order was being prepared and then I drove back to the car wash. By now the half hour had almost elapsed and the pair were due to return. I waited a little longer before concluding that they'd given me the slip.

'They've done it deliberately,' remarked Johnson, 'right at the beginning of our busiest period.'

On this occasion I was forced to agree with Johnson. No sooner had we finished our lunch than the flow of cars into the yard began to increase. Johnson handled the jet wash while I polished windscreens, headlights and hubcaps. The details in the ledger would have to wait. Joseph, Matthew and Thomas again demonstrated their flexibility by swapping tasks when required and between us we just about kept on top of the work. It goes without saying that I cursed Gustav and Wolfgang for abandoning their posts. I was now going to have to find others to take their places and really I wasn't sure where to start. As luck would have it Ted Gresham came by a little earlier than usual to collect his share of the takings. When he saw that we were undermanned he rolled up his sleeves and pitched in. He soon proved to be unafraid of hard work, just as I'd guessed the first time I laid eyes on him. In addition to showing us a better technique for achieving a cleaner windscreen he also suggested we gave vehicles a brief visual appraisal to check for faulty brake lights and so forth. He assured us that customers would appreciate these little extras. They were lessons well learnt and I looked forward to putting them into practice. As the afternoon drew to a close, however, Ted became noticeably irritable. Seemingly he was far from satisfied with what he'd seen. I'd been hoping to discuss with him my idea of a waiting room with complimentary coffee and pastries but instead I was led into the office and given a sharp dressing down.

'Why are you running the place short-handed?' he snapped. 'Trying to save yourself some money?'

'No,' I said. 'I simply had a few manpower difficulties this afternoon.'

'That's an understatement if ever I heard one.'

Ted picked up the ledger from the desk and began leafing through the pages. I then realised that I hadn't made any entries during the afternoon because of the unforeseen rush.

'How come this page is blank?'

'Sorry,' I said. 'I haven't had time to fill it in.'

'Well, you're going to have to make time,' he said. 'If I don't see any improvement very soon I'm afraid I'll have to get somebody else in.'

I glanced out of the window. The last customer of the day had now departed and Joseph, Matthew and Thomas had taken the opportunity to go to their corner and pray. Ted followed my gaze and for a moment I thought he might angrily ban such activities from taking place on the premises. To my surprise, though, he turned out to be more tolerant than I expected.

'You should be thankful you've got those three,' he remarked. 'If I were you I should do my best to hold onto them.'

We divided the day's takings and then he repeated his insistence that I provide a full quota of labour.

'You've got a week to buck yourself up,' he informed me before driving away.

When we got back to the fairground that evening we discovered that Gustav and Wolfgang had been and collected their meagre possessions. I presumed they must have cadged a ride there from a passing motorist. They'd left behind two sets of overalls: pale blue with a silver streak. This told me they had no intention of ever returning to the car wash.

The positive side of their sudden departure was that Joseph, Matthew, Thomas and myself now had a little more space in the brick hut. After the trauma of the afternoon I needed a beer so I left the three of them to their own devices and headed for The Wheatsheaf.

It was quiet when I got there and I was pleased to see that Eva was on duty behind the bar. Her manner was courteous verging on friendly. After she'd pulled me a pint of the usual I went and sat at the corner table and tried to work out how I could resolve my manpower problem. Briefly I considered trying the protest camp: perhaps I could offer Harcourt and Kingsnorth a job. When I thought about it properly, however, the plan seemed doomed to failure. The pair of them had very high ideals about their potential contribution to society and would no doubt view working in a car wash as very much beneath them. As regards the other people at the protest camp, few had looked to me as if they were seeking employment. The exception, of course, was Tamara but she already had three jobs and probably wouldn't have any time to spare. When I studied the customers ranged around the pub I could see nobody who appeared a likely candidate for the sort of work on offer. As a matter of fact they all seemed relatively prosperous. Ultimately I decided to make the most of my current team while keeping a general lookout for possible new recruits.

Standing at the bar was a man I recognised as a member of Frank's quiz team. His beer, apparently, was a source of dissatisfaction. He paid for it but then stood gazing into his glass with a gloomy expression.

'Sorry,' said Eva. 'Is it a bit cloudy?'

(She'd learnt a lot about beer during her brief tenure.)

'No,' said the man. 'It looks fine.'

'What's wrong with it then?'

'It's not entirely full.'

'Oh, sorry.'

'At the price they charge in here for a pint it should be full.'

'Yes,' said Eva. 'I quite agree.'

She took the glass and topped it up.

'Now there's too much head on it,' said the man.

Eva made a further adjustment and after thanking her profusely he finally took the beer away. After that the place began to get fairly busy. Norman went around collecting empty glasses and then took over from Eva while she had her break. As was her custom she came and sat beside me with a large glass of wine in her hand.

'Does that happen very often?' I enquired. 'About the not-quite-full pint?'

'Oh, all the time,' she said. 'They're never content with what they've got.'

'Well, the beer is rather expensive.'

Eva fixed me with a penetrating gaze.

'You ought to be careful,' she remarked at length. 'You might turn into one of them.'

'You mean one of the natives?'

'Yes.'

She drank a little of her wine.

'The people of this country,' she said, 'wallow in a kind of national disgruntlement. It's never ending and what makes it worse is that they don't even know what they're disgruntled about. Not really. Most of their grievances are trifling and when you provide a remedy they thank you so profusely it almost sounds like an apology. Yet it's the very triviality of their complaints that's the root of their troubles. It's a mild version of death by a thousand cuts. There are no huge intractable problems here like starvation, warfare, slavery, disease, tidal waves, pestilence, droughts, cyclones, volcanoes or earthquakes. Instead, they suffer a stream of minor irritations: they see other people avoiding taxes, other people being given empty houses, other people taking all the jobs, other people not queueing up properly, or failing to return their library books, or getting away with parking their cars in the wrong place, or breaking the speed limit, or cycling through red traffic lights. All this is compounded because the southerners think the northerners are always whingeing and the northerners believe that they alone do the hardest jobs. The northerners won't accept that there are factories, mills and coal mines in the south and the southerners think all northerners speak with the same accent. The majority of the population have never visited any other countries beyond their beaches. When they're abroad they deliberately get sunburnt despite the risks and they're enraged if they come home and learn that the weather's been nice while they were away. Finally, of course, they won't admit that foreign football teams are better than their own and they claim all defeats are due to cheating. Like I said: it's death by a thousand cuts.'

'And you think I'm becoming like them?'

'Yes.'

'I didn't realise.'

'It can't be helped,' she conceded. 'I probably am as well.'

After a pause I asked her what Johnson was doing this evening.

'He's filling in his application form for that job he saw in the newspaper.'

'If he gets it I'll be another man short at the car wash.'

'You'd better hope he doesn't then, hadn't you?'

With that she finished her wine and returned to her work.

Later, when I got back to the fairground, I found Joseph, Matthew and Thomas all fast asleep in the brick hut. In their usual considerate manner they'd laid out my bedding and left me a bedtime glass of milk beside my bunk. When I awoke next morning there was no sign of them. With some urgency I checked to see whether they were praying next to the electricity pylon in full view of passing trains. Fortunately they weren't. I then found a note from Joseph informing me that they'd gone in search of somewhere more discreet. They would meet me at the van. I'd left it in the lay-by on the main road so after a quick wash I walked up and found them waiting for me.

'Did you find anywhere suitable?' I enquired.

'Yes, sir,' said Joseph. 'We are very flexible.'

I didn't ask for any further details, mainly because I was distracted by a number of vehicles that had begun pulling into the lay-by. There were several lorries laden with all kinds of construction materials as well as some minibuses full of men in orange high-visibility jackets. One of the drivers asked if I'd be moving the van anytime soon.

'Yes,' I said. 'Right now actually.'

'Thanks.'

'Are you going to be working around here?'

'Yes,' he said. 'It's quite a big project.'

We set off for the cafe and during the journey we passed some more minibuses coming the other way plus a lorry carrying a bulldozer. Given its location I guessed the project must have some connection with the railways. Oddly enough, though, none of the vehicles bore the RAILWAY PROPERTY BOARD insignia. As a matter of fact they had a very anonymous look about them as they went rolling past: in consequence the exact nature of the project remained obscure. Still, I concluded, no doubt I'd be able to see for myself in the days to come.

15

The first people I spotted when I entered the cafe were Kevin and Pete. They were sitting in the opposite corner to the eggs, chips and beans table looking rather sorry for themselves.

'Oh, morning,' I said, with some surprise. 'I didn't notice your van outside.'

'That's because it's been impounded,' said Kevin.

'Why?'

'Unpaid fines and penalty charges. Assorted.'

'We had no idea we'd even incurred them,' added Pete. 'It's left us in a bit of a fix. We were totally dependent on that van.'

'Yes, I imagine you were.'

Under the circumstances I felt it would be appropriate to buy them a mug of tea apiece. I invited them to join me at the eggs, chips and beans table and they reluctantly complied. They plainly weren't accustomed to sitting there and looked a little uncomfortable at first. When I went to the counter to order my breakfast a sudden thought occurred to me.

'Have either of you eaten?' I enquired.

It transpired that they'd only had a bowl of cornflakes each so I ordered the full complement of eggs, chips and beans plus bread and butter to accompany the mugs of tea. Eva served it all up and once the table was laden Kevin and Pete began to look a little happier.

'So what are you up to nowadays?' Pete asked.

'I'm running a car wash,' I said. 'It's in that yard where Bob Twigg was based.'

'Don't talk to us about Bob Twigg,' uttered Kevin. 'The bane of our lives.'

'Really?' I said. 'I've always found him very pleasant to deal with.'

'Actually to be fair,' said Pete, 'Bob himself is fine. It's his wife who's the nightmare. She handles all the finances.'

'Is that why you had a cash flow problem?'

'Correct.'

We finished our breakfast in silence and I wondered if I should ask the obvious question. I knew it might dent their pride but in reality it would be of benefit to all three of us.

'I don't suppose,' I said at last, 'that you'd consider working in a car wash?'

'We'd consider anything at present to be honest,' said Kevin.

'Well, can you start today?'

'Yep.'

I told them the rates of pay and they accepted at once. By this time Johnson had made an appearance. When I introduced him to his new workmates he adopted a rather supercilious air.

'Ah, yes,' he said, eyeing Kevin and Pete with barely disguised derision. 'We've met before.'

He then sat down at a neighbouring table and began leafing through his newspaper.

'How did you get on with that job application?' I enquired.

'I haven't heard back from them yet.'

'What job was that then?' said Kevin.

'Johnson's applied for work in the public domain.'

'Don't broadcast it to everyone!' Johnson hissed. 'It's meant to be kept secret.'

'Since when?' I asked.

'It said on the application form: discretion must be exercised. I'm not allowed to discuss it with other people.'

'Most likely government agency work,' said Kevin. 'They keep it all quiet because they're doing it on the cheap. They're so desperate to fill the posts that they'll take virtually anybody.'

'Is that so?' said Johnson.

'Very low qualification requirements from what I've heard.'

'Well, maybe you should apply then.'

It struck me that Johnson and Kevin weren't getting off to a very good start seeing that they were going to be working together all day. When we went out to the van I realised I would need to be careful in the allocation of the front seats. Fortunately Joseph, Matthew and Thomas were their usual smiling selves. They made such a fuss welcoming Kevin and Pete that the pair were more or less obliged to join them in the back of the van. Johnson took the front seat and I drove us all to the yard.

It didn't take Kevin and Pete long to adapt to the work. I decided that Johnson would now be permanently in charge of the jet wash while the two 'new boys' could look after windscreens, hubcaps and headlights. They liked the idea of the daily payment and at lunchtime volunteered to go and collect the fish and chips.

When they saw Joseph, Matthew and Thomas praying in their corner they remarked that the practise was common in every workplace these days but offered no opinion on the matter. By the end of the first afternoon they'd awarded them the nickname 'The Three Valeteers'. There was some occasional light-hearted 'joshing' but it was entirely good-natured.

Johnson, on the other hand, was becoming very difficult to manage. I'd noticed in the cafe that he largely ignored Eva as she went about her work and now he was being similarly remote with the rest of us. If the car wash got busy he refused to help with the other tasks despite my threat that it would impair his productivity bonus. He no longer seemed to care and I sensed he was simply biding his time while he waited for his job application to be processed. He'd evidently staked a lot on it and I assumed this explained his testy manner.

Casually I pondered what the work might entail. Information was rather vague beyond the fact that it was in the public domain. I'd actually gone to the trouble of writing down the phone number in the advertisement just in case. To tell the truth, though, I wasn't particularly interested.

When Ted Gresham dropped by in the late afternoon I could see he was very pleased that we were back in full swing again. Apparently he, Kevin and Pete were slightly acquainted. They gave one another nods of recognition as he crossed the yard into the office and he commented that I'd assembled a good team. We divided the takings and then I prepared to close up for the evening.

I was just trying to work out who should have precedence in the front of the van when Ted announced that he knew roughly where Kevin and Pete lived and could give them a lift part of the way home. He also promised to provide each of them with a brand new set of overalls. All three of them were deep in conversation as they climbed into his car and drove off.

'I meant to ask you,' said Johnson. 'Will you be in The Wheatsheaf tonight?'

'Probably,' I replied. 'Why do you want to know?'

'Eva has a proposition for you.'
'Do you know what it is?'
'No.'

'Okay, I'll try and have a word with her later.'

Joseph, Matthew and Thomas were hovering nearby ready to leave.

'Do any of you want to sit in the front seat? I enquired. 'There's a spare place if you want it.'

After some consultation with his companions Joseph elected to join Johnson and me while the other two travelled in the back. We closed and locked the car wash before heading for the cafe. Half an hour later we dropped Johnson off and it was decided that both Matthew and Thomas could squeeze in the front with Joseph and me. They seemed to view this as a treat and we were all in a jolly mood as we continued home. On the way we passed a large convoy of lorries and minibuses travelling in the opposite direction. Plainly work on the 'big project' had been completed for the day.

Darkness was falling when at last we approached the railway arch. I slowed down and pulled into the lay-by. It took me a moment to recognise the place because during our absence everything had changed. There was now a high security fence running around the perimeter of the fairground. Ahead of us was a spiked steel gate bearing a sign:

NATIONAL RECEPTION AND PROCESSING CENTRE
STAGE TWO

To my surprise Joseph, Matthew and Thomas took one look at the sign and then went into an absolute panic. Instantly they threw open the passenger door and began scrambling out of the van. Joseph was last to go. He turned to me with a wild expression on his face.

'Traitor!' he cried. 'You've betrayed us!'

Without a further word the three of them ran off into the deepening shadows beyond the railway arch. I called after them but it was to no avail. After switching off the engine I sat in the van and peered through the windscreen at the former fairground. The transformation was all-encompassing. The two wooden posts, the galvanised chain and the concrete road had all gone: now there was just a wide tarmac strip. As far as I could see the expanse of scrubby undergrowth had all been cleared away. Just inside the gate stood a hut and there were further low-level buildings stretching beyond it. Each had a letter of the alphabet stencilled on its door.

In the failing light I saw that there were a couple of uniformed men sitting in the hut behind a window. I got out of the van and walked over to try and attract their attention. Eventually the door opened. One of the men emerged and came to speak to me through the gate.

'Sorry,' I said, 'but I left a few personal items in the brick hut down the bottom there.'

'Don't know anything about a brick hut,' he said. 'We had a bulldozer operating here today. It's all been flattened.'

I could tell by his accent that he wasn't a local man.

'Is the work finished?' I asked.

'Can't say really,' he replied.

'Do you happen to know what 'Stage Two' means?'

'Can't say really.'

Further questioning got me nowhere so I thanked him for his help and wished him good night. He returned to his hut. I then went and sat in the van and pondered the situation. It wasn't very good but there were one or two positives. Fortunately I had some money locked in the glove compartment. The weather wasn't too cold so for the time being I could sleep overnight in the van at a push. I wasn't sure where Joseph, Matthew and Thomas had run off to but I had a feeling I wouldn't see them at the car wash again. This meant that my workforce was now down to Johnson, Kevin, Pete and myself and it might be reduced even further if Johnson landed the job he'd applied for.

The thought occurred to me that Barry Barton wouldn't be very pleased when he learnt the fairground had been taken over. He was supposed to have long-standing rights of access to the place. Now these had seemingly been swept aside to build a new reception and processing centre. I had no idea whether this was intended as an alternative or an addition to the seaside facility. Whatever the reason, the work had been carried out in a great hurry and I couldn't help detecting a sense of urgency about it. The fact that the man at the gate was being so cagey didn't help matters. It was almost as though he'd been sworn to secrecy. For a while I considered driving to the protest camp to find out if Harcourt knew what was going on. In the event, however, I decided to go to the pub instead. As I departed a train trundled across the railway arch and along the far embankment. It was now totally dark which meant the passengers would have seen none of the changes down below them. The development was evidently important but how much the public knew or even cared was anybody's guess.

Eva was busy serving another customer when I entered The Wheatsheaf so it was Norman who pulled my pint. I glanced around and saw that Johnson was sitting at the same table as Frank and his team mates from the quiz night. They were deep in discussion. Johnson was listening closely to what Frank had to say to him and was writing various points in a small notebook. How this meeting had come about was unclear but I assumed that Johnson was trying to inveigle a place in the team. Or perhaps he was simply trying to pick up a few tips from the master of the game. Either way, he was distracted enough to be unaware of my presence. This in turn meant that I could enjoy a quiet pint at a table in the corner.

Johnson didn't even notice when Eva came and sat beside me with a glass of wine in her hand. I found it outrageous that he took her for granted but at the same time I was glad of her company.

I told her what had happened at the fairground.

'Sounds like a disaster,' she remarked.

'Hopefully it's just a temporary setback,' I said. 'It means I'll have to sleep in the van until I get sorted out.'

'In that case you may be interested in a proposition I have in mind.'

'Oh yes?'

'How would you like to rent the spare room of my flat?'

I hesitated to answer. In most circumstances I would have jumped at the opportunity to move into some proper accommodation. What made me wary, however, were the present domestic arrangements. To be more precise I found the idea of Eva and Johnson being together in another room in the same flat rather unsettling. For this reason I decided to hedge a little.

'So it's vacant is it?'

'Well, obviously it's vacant,' she snapped. 'Otherwise I wouldn't have offered it to you, would I?'

'Suppose not.'

I asked her what the rent would be and then made some related enquiries about utility bills and so forth. Eva explained that they were all included.

'There's just one condition,' she added.

'Which is?'

'You'd have to share the room with Johnson.'

'Oh,' I said with surprise. 'I thought you...I mean...have you...er...does he know?'

'I haven't told him yet,' said Eva. 'I need your answer first.'

'Well, that certainly throws a different light on the matter.'

'Yes,' she said. 'I thought it would.'

Eva gave me an impenetrable gaze and I swiftly came to a decision.

'Okay, yes, I'll take the room then, thanks.'

'Not tonight, though,' she said.

'Alright.'

'I'll let you know when.'

With that she finished her wine and returned to work. The pub was gradually getting fuller. I peered across at Johnson and saw that he was still in close conference with Frank and the others. I was about to go and buy myself a second pint when Tamara emerged from the saloon bar. She was collecting empty glasses. When she spotted me she came over and paused briefly to talk.

'They've been expecting you at the protest camp,' she said. 'Harcourt thought you might go and offer your support.'

'Well, I would if I had time,' I replied, 'but I've been rather busy lately.'

Tamara regarded me coolly.

'Yes,' she said. 'That's most people's excuse.'

'Have there been some difficulties then?'

'Evidently you don't read the newspapers. People are allowed to leave the camp but they can't go back: the authorities have got them hemmed in with barbed wire.'

'Good grief.'

'Then they had the effrontery to offer Harcourt a job in this new government agency that's been set up.'

'You mean paid employment?'

'Yes.'

'Did he accept?'

'Of course he didn't accept!' she exclaimed. 'He's a man of principle!'

Tamara uttered these words with such passion that several customers turned to look at her. She flushed somewhat before lowering her voice.

'I haven't been able to get back into the camp for a week now,' she continued in an undertone. 'It's a desperate state of affairs. The strikers have been undermined by all those untrained personnel that the management keep bussing in and now the reception centre is moving to another location.'

'Any idea where?'

'No, but we'll find out soon enough.'

By now I was aware that Norman was eyeing Tamara sternly from behind the bar. He tapped his finger on an empty glass and she quickly resumed her duties. After she'd gone I thought about Harcourt's uncompromising stance and wondered how I would have reacted if I'd received a similar offer. Plainly it was an attempt to buy him off: undoubtedly the protest camp would collapse without his leadership.

The rest of the evening was uneventful. Tamara more or less ignored me as she went around the tables and Eva was fully-occupied behind the bar. I'd taken the precaution of parking the van in a quiet street about half a mile away. At closing time I slipped unnoticed out of the pub.

Next morning I woke at seven and headed for the cafe to collect Johnson. As soon as I got there Eva came out to inform me that he'd already gone off in another vehicle.

'It was a grey van,' she said. 'I saw it through the window. It kept bibbing its horn.'

'He must have started his new job.'

'Yes.'

'Well, he could have let me know,' I said. 'This is going to leave me short-handed again.'

'He didn't even tell me,' she replied. 'The first I knew about it was when the alarm clock went off in the spare room.'

I went inside and sat down at the eggs, chips and beans table. Eva seemed to understand my predicament and offered to discreetly ask other customers if they knew of anyone immediately available for work. Despite her efforts there was nobody forthcoming so at seven thirty I paid for my breakfast and headed for the car wash. When I arrived I found the double gates wide open. Kevin and Pete were already inside cleaning the first vehicle of the day. They were both wearing crisp new overalls: pale blue with a silver streak.

'Ted gave us the spare key to the yard,' said Kevin, 'so we thought we might as well get started.'

'Did he drop you off here this morning?' I enquired.

'Yes, he's been very obliging actually.'

I went over to the office and took the ledger out of the drawer. I wanted to demonstrate that I was still in charge of the car wash so I sat at the desk and made the appropriate entry. The reality of the situation, however, meant that I would have little time for lounging in the office. There were now only three of us to deal with all the vehicles that were coming through and I wanted to make sure we kept on top of the work. I explained to Kevin and Pete that their other colleagues were absent for personal reasons. Therefore I wanted Kevin to operate the jet wash while I looked after windscreens, headlights and hub caps. Pete would be in charge of valeting.

'But there were three of them doing it yesterday,' he protested. 'It's not fair to put me on my own.'

'Can't be helped for the time being,' I said. 'Just think of the productivity bonus you'll be earning.'

We worked hard all morning and when lunchtime came I sent Pete off to buy some fish and chips. I was hoping against hope that Ted Gresham wouldn't turn up and see us struggling to cope but in fact that was exactly what happened. At about three in the afternoon he made a sudden appearance and again buckled down to help us get through the rush. I knew, though, that some form of reckoning was unavoidable. Sure enough, when early evening came and the flow of customers had finally tailed off, Ted called me into the office.

'We can't go on like this,' he said. 'You're just not managing to hold a workforce together.'

'I thought you'd given me a week to sort it out,' I replied.

'That's what I said initially, yes, but it's even worse today than last time. Sorry but I've had a bit of a rethink. Kevin told me he knows some people who could join the team straightaway so I've decided to put him in charge.'

'What about my percentage?'

'Well, I'll pay you your share for today but that'll be the end of it I'm afraid.'

'So I'm getting the sack, am I?'

'No, of course not,' Ted replied, 'but from now on you'll be working for Kevin.'

16

The lights of the cafe were still on when I pulled up outside. The place was completely empty but still it looked warm and inviting. The sign on the door said OPEN so I went in and sat down at the eggs, chips and beans table.

A moment later Eva appeared.

'Wouldn't you like something different for a change?' she enquired.

'You mean different from eggs, chips and beans?'

'Yes.'

'Not if it means moving to another table.'

'No need to be churlish.'

'Sorry.'

It transpired that Eva had been left in charge of the cafe while the owner went to the cash-and-carry to stock up. She then announced that if I didn't mind waiting she'd go to the kitchen and rustle me up a nice supper. I told her about being short-handed at the car wash and she was sympathetic.

'You can't rely on Johnson,' she said. 'Nobody can.'

'Well, I'm going to have a severe word with him when he comes back from work,' I said. 'He let me down badly this morning.'

'Oh, I don't think he's coming back,' said Eva. 'I've had a look in the spare room and all his stuff has gone.'

'Well, he didn't have much to begin with.'

'He's got even less now.'

'Same here.'

After supper she closed the cafe and I helped her to do the washing up. She then took me up to her flat to see the spare room. I changed out of my overalls and had a shower.

'Working at the pub later?' I enquired.

'No,' said Eva. 'I've got the night off.'

'Traffic warden duties?'

'No.'

'Can I buy you a drink then?'

'Yes, but we'll go to a different pub.'

Eva knew the area better than me. She said there was a popular pub down near the seafront if I was prepared to drive. I thought it would be interesting to try the place so we soon headed off. It gave me an odd feeling having Eva as a passenger in my van, especially when I recalled the occasion she'd issued me with a parking ticket. That was for the other van, of course, and it occurred to me that Kevin and Pete would soon be in a position to pay their fines and get it back on the road. Hopefully their fortunes would then be fully restored. I wished them luck. I didn't really resent them for taking charge of the car wash so rapidly: actually it relieved me of the burden of responsibility. From now on I could just be an ordinary worker without a care in the world.

The pub in question was called The Cross Hands. It was busy with a friendly crowd of people and I was pleased to see they served the same range of beer as The Wheatsheaf. I bought a pint for myself while Eva chose a glass of wine. We sat down at a table near a window. Some customers were playing darts and there was a poster on the wall for a forthcoming tournament. A little later I spotted Mr Alder from the deckchair hut. He was sitting all alone at the bar with a half empty glass. For a moment I was tempted to go over and say hello. I'd been in this country long enough, however, to learn that such gestures were considered unnecessary. At most I should give him a nod of acknowledgement if he happened to notice me. Nothing more was required. People didn't make a fuss of each other here. Actually the opposite was true: whenever possible they pretended other people didn't exist.

Naturally Eva understood all this. She sat quietly beside me and appeared to take pleasure in my company. By the end of the evening I'd told her everything I'd done since I'd arrived. She insisted on buying the second round of drinks and when last orders were called I bought the third. Eva had another glass of wine while I opted for a coca-cola. It was all most enjoyable and then we went and wandered along the seafront.

'Would you like to see our boat?' I asked. 'It should be down there by the breakwater.'

'Alright,' said Eva.

In the light of the moon I led her down the steps and onto the beach. There was a light breeze blowing and we could hear waves breaking in the distance. Seemingly the tide was a long way out. I couldn't quite remember the exact location of the breakwater but we kept going and ultimately it loomed out of the darkness. The boat, however, had gone.

'Ah,' I said. 'Sorry about that. Somebody must have been and salvaged it.'

Eva smiled.

'I suppose that means you're stuck here forever.'

'Looks like it.'

We walked back to the van and then I drove us to the flat. All was in darkness as we entered and when Eva switched the light on we saw a door key lying on the mat. Evidently Johnson had returned it.

'Nice of him,' remarked Eva. 'Unusually considerate actually.'

She handed the spare key to me and then we went upstairs. Eva didn't believe in late night coffee so we both prepared for bed.

'You can use the bathroom first,' she said. 'I'll wait.'

The spare room was sparse to say the least. There were no sheets or blankets but I was quite content to settle for an eiderdown that I found in a cupboard. I closed the door and got into bed. For a while I could hear Eva padding around in the narrow corridor between the rooms and then finally her door clicked shut. I closed my eyes and tried to go to sleep. The flat was very quiet and it should have been easy but actually it wasn't. I lay on my side and then on my back and then on my side again. Time was passing but sleep remained elusive. A distant clock struck two. I was still awake an hour later when Eva's voice came drifting through to me from her bedroom.

'If you stay there any longer,' she said, 'I'll have to give you a parking ticket.'

17

When I arrived at the yard the following day Kevin was busily organising a new contingent of workers. There were three of them (Dave, Gaz and Kenny) and I got the immediate impression that they'd all known Kevin and Pete for years. During the morning I heard a lot of jokes and references that I didn't really understand but which had the rest of them falling about with laughter. There was also a great deal of horseplay. For a while they tended to regard the jet wash as a kind of toy and kept using it to splash each other (and occasionally me). Finally, however, Kevin managed to establish a semblance of discipline and the business began functioning properly. Needless to say I felt a little like an outsider, especially when he gave me the job of valeting the cars. As Pete had pointed out the previous day this was really a task for three people and at first I struggled with it. I had no intention of complaining, though, as it might be interpreted as a sign of weakness. Kevin maintained the custom of going out at lunchtime to buy fish and chips and when he returned I noticed that he'd chosen cod for me and plaice for all the others. There was no daily cash allowance but again I said nothing.

As the afternoon passed I realised that the new set-up was much less efficient than before. The newcomers spent a lot of time chatting to one another. Any excuse and the work ground to a halt. In consequence the queue of cars at the gate gradually lengthened. For some reason Ted Gresham didn't pay his usual visit so he failed to witness the backlog for himself. Otherwise I was sure he would have reversed his decision about who should be in charge. The last few customers were actually turned away. Apparently there was a football match that Kevin and the others wanted to watch so it was relatively early when they closed down for the evening.

'We'll be getting our van back tomorrow,' Kevin informed me. 'Would you be able to give us a lift home tonight?'

'I suppose so,' I said. 'Where to exactly?'

When he told me I knew at once that the journey would take me considerably out of my way. Still, I'd already agreed to his request so all five piled into the van (Kevin and Pete sat in the front). It took quite a while to drop everyone off at their homes and it was dark when I got back to the cafe.

I shared with Eva my misgivings about how the car wash was being run.

'Very unproductive,' I concluded. 'All any of them are interested in is what time they finish work.'

'Perhaps you should try a different job.'

'Yes, but what?'

'You could be a traffic warden.'

'Oh no,' I said. 'That would be against my principles.'

'What principles are those then?'

'Well, you know: defying the forces of oppression.'

Eva laughed out loud.

'Traffic wardens aren't the forces of oppression!' she said. 'They're just as put upon as everyone else!'

'Alright then,' I said. 'Defying the forces of exploitation.'

She shook her head sadly.

'That's the sort of nonsense Johnson kept spouting. I'm surprised to hear it coming from you. Exploitation is just an economic reality. The simple fact is that some individuals are better at making money than others. As for oppression, well, people in this country don't know the meaning of the word. There's no oppression here. Not really. Not like in other countries.'

'So you don't think there'll ever be a revolution?'

'Certainly not. They had one a few hundred years ago and it changed nothing.'

'All the same,' I said, 'I'm not very keen to be a traffic warden. From what I've heard they're hardly popular around here.'

Eva eyed me coolly.

'Yourself excepted, of course.'

'What about that job Johnson's taken?' she suggested. 'They're still seeking applicants.'

'Not sure,' I said. 'This new government agency sounds rather shady.'

'Perhaps he's joined the forces of oppression.'

'I wouldn't put it past him.'

'No, nor me.'

A little later Eva set off for an evening's work in the pub. I offered to give her a lift there in the van but she preferred the self-reliance of her moped.

'Don't forget it's quiz night,' she said. 'Will you be taking part?'

'No,' I said, 'but I quite enjoy being a neutral observer.'

'Okay, see you later.'

I fancied a few pints so in the end I decided to walk to The Wheatsheaf. When I arrived the preparations for the quiz were just getting underway. Jerry was going around the various tables distributing answer sheets and there was a tangible buzz of anticipation building up amongst the customers. Norman poured me a pint and I was just pondering where to sit when Johnson walked in with three other men. He politely directed them to a corner table and I got the impression that they were all fairly new acquaintances. Moreover they appeared unfamiliar with the inside of a pub. They sat gazing around them as Johnson asked what they would like to drink. Evidently he now had money in his pocket. He went to the bar and I was quite pleased when Eva avoided serving him. He placed an order with Norman instead and while he stood waiting his eyes fell on me. I gave him a nod but he ignored me completely. Once he'd returned to his table he was approached by Jerry who enquired if he needed an answer sheet. To judge by his positive response this was the sole reason he'd come to The Wheatsheaf. I guessed he'd assembled a team from amongst his new work colleagues and had come in search of victory. Obviously to achieve this he would have to overcome Frank and his redoubtable acolytes. They happened to be sitting at a neighbouring table and two or three times I saw Johnson and Frank engaged in amiable discussion. I could tell, however, that once the quiz began the friendly banter would cease.

A little later Jerry plugged in his microphone. The quiz was the usual blend of popular culture and sport with only a sporadic smattering of general knowledge. I perched on a bar stool and listened with interest.

It turned out to be a particularly difficult quiz for Johnson. On several occasions during the course of the evening he interrupted to ask if a question could be rephrased (in most cases it couldn't), to check whether he'd heard it correctly (mostly he hadn't) or if the subsequent answer could be independently verified. I suspected early on that Johnson's team was struggling and he was using these queries as a kind of distraction. Soon his conduct began to irritate the other participants and after many complaints he eventually received a sharp reprimand from Jerry. After that he sullenly wrote down his answers without consulting any of his team mates. They in turn sat at their table in bewildered silence. Not one of them offered to go and buy another round of drinks and when the quiz came to an end all four were still sitting there with empty glasses. Johnson's gambit had failed spectacularly and he departed the pub before the final results were even read out. His three associates followed him into the night.

Frank's team won, naturally, and in the aftermath Eva came and spoke to me.

'I don't think we'll be seeing Johnson again.'

'I'm not so sure,' I remarked. 'He has a pronounced tendency to bounce back.'

I ordered another pint and sat reflecting on what I'd seen. It struck me that none of Johnson's colleagues had appeared very worldly-wise. In fact they were more like automatons. If indeed they had enrolled in some shiny new government agency then it's prospects seemed bleak. I decided, therefore, that I would definitely not be applying for a job. Instead, I'd carry on working at the car wash and see what happened.

Later, when I was walking back to the flat, Eva passed me on her moped and beeped her horn. By the time I got home she was asleep.

The following morning, before going downstairs to open the cafe, she asked me for my share of the rent.

'Oh, sorry,' I said. 'I was planning to pay you at the end of the week.'

'Have you spent all your money then?'

'Well, I've got just about enough for breakfast and lunch.'

'I thought the car wash paid a daily cash allowance.'

'When I was in charge of the place, yes,' I affirmed, 'but it's been discontinued now.'

Eva was highly displeased. It transpired that Johnson had barely contributed to the rent and now it seemed I was no different. I assured her that I would press Kevin about a cash advance as soon as I got to work but she remained unconvinced. A little later, when she served my breakfast, there was no butter on my bread.

I arrived at the car wash feeling just as detached as I had the day before. I'd made an effort to get there early but Kevin, Pete, Dave, Gaz and Kenny had beaten me to it. The other van was already parked in the yard which meant there was no room for mine. I had to leave it further along the road.

Even so I did my best to be cheerful. I walked in through the gates and saw Kevin standing in the office doorway.

'Morning,' I said (cheerfully). 'I see you've got your van back at last.'

'No thanks to you, though,' he replied. 'You incurred three separate penalty charges.'

'Oh, sorry.'

'Cost us a fortune.'

'Yes, I suppose it did.'

'So we'll have to deduct it from your wages.'

He went on to inform me that they were only keeping me on at the car wash to make sure they got their money back. Getting a cash advance, therefore, was plainly out of the question. I realised I had no real choice except to try and work my way out of my predicament.

I toiled throughout the morning for practically no reward (apart from a couple of gratuities from appreciative customers). Pete and the others persisted in treating me as an outsider but thankfully I was still included in the lunchtime fish and chip run.

'Plaice and chips?' Kevin enquired.

Evidently he was feeling generous. Or maybe he remembered my kindness to Pete and him when I bought their breakfasts in the cafe. Either way I became aware of a slight softening of his attitude as the day progressed. It must have gradually dawned on Kevin that I needed some kind of incentive to keep me going and a little later he called me into the office.

'I've been having a think,' he said. 'It's quite harsh deducting all that money from your wages.'

'Yes, it is a bit,' I agreed.

'So why don't you let us have the van back in full settlement of your debt?'

The suggestion came as a surprise and it took a few moments for its full meaning to sink in.

'But how would I get to and from work?' I enquired at length.

'Well, we can drop you off at the cafe tonight,' he said, 'but after that you'll have to get here under your own steam.'

I pondered the proposition. Over the recent weeks I'd become rather attached to that van. It was nice to drive and whenever I was behind the wheel I always enjoyed the sensation of unbound freedom that it gave me. The thought occurred to me, however, that I was no longer responsible for conveying a workforce back and forth. Therefore, I didn't really need a van any more. I could probably manage with a car or maybe a moped like Eva's. Or conceivably even a bicycle. If parting with the van meant I would receive a full wage packet at the end of each week then it was perhaps a price worth paying. I was confident I'd be able to get my finances back on a level footing fairly quickly. In the meantime I would simply have to rise a little earlier in the morning and walk to work.

'Alright,' I said, handing Kevin the keys. 'It's a deal.'

He seemed more than satisfied with the arrangement and immediately went out into the yard to tell Pete. I took the opportunity to have a quick glance through the ledger. Straightaway I saw that it contained several inaccuracies. During the morning we'd washed and valeted a good many cars but according to the ledger we'd only done half a dozen. Apparently Kevin (most likely with Pete's connivance) was operating some kind of fiddle. Still, it was no longer my concern so I closed the ledger and returned to my work station.

Just as the afternoon drew to a close a van pulled up opposite the double gates. It was grey in colour and bore no identifying markings. We'd just finished washing a car and I was busy cleaning inside with the vacuum cleaner. I glanced out and saw Kevin strolling across to speak to the occupants of the van. He then directed them up the road to the nearest parking space. A few seconds later he strode quickly across the yard and signalled me to join him. He had a look of urgency about him so I scrambled out of the car.

'You'd better scarper,' he said. 'Those geezers are from that new government agency. They'll be coming back in a minute.'

'Are they after me then?' I asked.

'They're after anyone who's not registered.'

'Well, I've got nothing to hide,' I said. 'I'll wait and see what they have to say.'

Kevin gazed at me in utter disbelief.

'Don't be a cunt all your life,' he said. 'Have a day off.'

I wasn't sure what he meant by this remark. He shook his head in a resigned manner before turning away and retreating to the office. I finished the car I was working on and then paused for a rest. Next moment three uniformed men entered the yard. Pete was standing nearby. They spoke briefly to him and he gave an indifferent shrug. They then approached Dave, Gaz and Kenny who were similarly non-committal. None of them, it appeared, were prepared to cooperate with the newcomers. I wondered whether they were trying to protect me or simply displaying a general contempt for the new government agency. Either way I realised I had nowhere to hide.

I wandered over to the men.

'Looking for someone in particular?' I enquired.

'We're looking for anybody who isn't registered,' said one of them.

I knew instantly from his accent that he wasn't a local man. He wore the same uniform as the man I'd spoken to at the reception centre.

'Yes, well,' I said. 'I suppose that's me.'

'You need to come and register.'

'Has the strike finished then?'

'You need to come and register.'

'Am I under arrest?'

'No, but you need to come and register.'

Casually I debated how many times he would repeat his mantra. He didn't seem to have much else to say. Resistance was clearly futile, however, so I accompanied the men to their van. As I left the yard my workmates were already preparing the next car for the wash. None of them even glanced in my direction.

18

When the back doors of the van were opened I discovered that I wasn't the only passenger. There were four other men and two women. One of the men was wearing the distinctive yellow and green boiler suit I'd seen on several occasions in the cafe. Both women had sulky expressions.

There was a bulkhead between the forward part of the van and the rear. It was fitted with an observation window. The three uniformed men slammed the doors shut and then climbed into the front. Casually I speculated whether they enjoyed their work or not. They hadn't been particularly hostile or unpleasant in their attitude and they certainly had no air of corporate indoctrination about them. I suspected that at heart they were probably little different from me. After all, they were patently a very long way from home just the same as I was. It was only their job that was different. For some reason this made me feel a little better.

After we'd been travelling for a while I peered through the observation window and at once recognised the route we were taking. Another half a mile and we would be going straight past the cafe! When we got a bit nearer I tapped on the glass. The three men in the front of the van ignored me. I tapped again. No response. When I tapped for a third time the van juddered to a halt. A few seconds later the back door opened and one of the men looked in.

'Why do you keep tapping on the glass?' he demanded.

'Well,' I said, 'I was going to ask if I could pop in and speak to my girlfriend for a moment. She'll be wondering where I am.'

'Out of the question,' he said. 'You need to come and register.'

'And then I can go home, can I?'

He didn't answer the question. Instead, he slammed the door and we continued on our journey. By now it was clear that we were heading for the National Reception and Processing Centre (Stage Two). I experienced a very peculiar feeling as we approached the railway arch and slowed down. This was the exact spot where Barry Barton had held his annual funfair yet now it was surrounded by a high security fence. The steel gate was closed but when the driver hooted the horn a man emerged from his hut and opened it. (Through the observation window I saw that it was the man I'd spoken to other day.) Half a minute later we pulled up outside a low-level building with the letter A stencilled on its door. There was a brief delay before we were let out of the van and then our names were taken. Darkness was falling as the seven of us stood around waiting to see what happened next. It was a tedious few minutes. Ever since I'd joined them the two sulky women had been complaining to each other in a language I didn't understand and their whining tone was now beginning to irritate me. It transpired that the cause of the delay had been a missing key. Finally it was located and the door was unlocked. The lights were switched on and as we entered I was struck by an overwhelming smell of fresh paint. Seemingly we were the first people to arrive since the building's completion. The men in uniform appeared to know little more about the layout of the place than we did and it was only after a further delay that we were at last led along a corridor and into a waiting room. There were about twenty chairs available.

The two women sat together but all the men spaced themselves out.

Another quarter of an hour went by and then we heard a faint rattling noise coming along the corridor. The door to the waiting room swung open and an elderly lady came in wheeling a tea trolley.

'Tea and biscuits anyone?' she asked.

'Ooh, yes please,' I said. 'I haven't had anything for hours.'

Despite being the only person to speak up I had to wait until she'd been around all the others first. She slowly pushed her trolley along the line of chairs and I watched in dismay as the supply of biscuits gradually diminished.

'It's supposed to be one each,' she confided to the man in the yellow and green boiler suit, 'but you look as if you need feeding up a bit.'

She gave him a couple of extra biscuits. Another man also received a double ration and by the time she got to me she'd run out.

'There are some more in my cupboard,' she reassured me. 'I'll go and get them.'

It took her a long while to come back and by the time she returned I'd drunk my tea.

'Sorry, dear,' she said. 'I had to find some steps to stand on and reach them down.'

By way of apology she slipped me several biscuits and gave me a refill. I thanked her and asked if she knew when we would be attended to.

'Are you here to register?' she enquired.

'Yes.'

'Well, you have to have an interview first. It's a very nice man who does them. Probably won't be long now.'

I thanked her again and she wheeled her trolley out of the waiting room. She left the door open and for the next half hour or so I heard occasional footsteps going by in the corridor. Eventually I moved to a chair opposite the door so that I could possibly catch a glimpse of anybody passing. It was all starting to get a bit tiresome: apart from a small pile of photographic magazines (which the two sulky women had already monopolised) there was nothing to help pass the time.

After another hour, however, there were more footsteps. I glanced towards the corridor and saw Johnson go walking past. Quickly I went to the doorway and called his name. He turned to face me, gave me a nod of acknowledgement and then put his finger to his lips conspiratorially before vanishing through another door. I interpreted this as a hopeful sign so I returned to my chair and ignored the quizzical looks I received from the other people in the waiting room. Obviously I'd had my ups and downs with Johnson but as a compatriot I felt certain I could rely on him to get me through the registration process reasonably smoothly.

Within minutes there was further activity in the building and finally a loudspeaker crackled into life. A name was called and directed to go to room 3. Instantly one of the women rose to her feet and went out. The other woman was called next (room 3 again) and then the first of the men (room 2). Now that it was underway the process seemed to be moving fairly quickly. As my turn approached I began to rehearse what I might say during the interview. I wanted to explain that I'd come to this country to try and help cure the people of their disgruntlement but I'd since discovered that actually no cure was required. It had been made clear to me over the past few weeks that disgruntlement was their natural condition and that they would never wish it otherwise. Furthermore, the state of national disgruntlement rendered the country infinitely more interesting than other countries and therefore I would like to apply for citizenship. I was confident my deposition would be sufficient to get me through the interview.

Soon there were only two of us waiting: me and the man in the yellow and green boiler suit. We got chatting and he told me he'd been working as a tyre fitter when he was picked up.

'Were you at the place with all the northerners?' I enquired.

'Yes,' he said, 'mainly northerners but a few others from further afield too.'

'Was there someone called Johnson there? Left a few weeks ago?'

'Don't talk to me about Johnson. He nearly got us all sacked.'

'Complaining about being exploited?'

'Yes, that was him.'

At that moment the man's name was called over the loudspeaker. We wished each other luck, shook hands and then he was gone.

I waited a little longer and finally I heard my own name. I was directed to room 1. It was at the end of the corridor. The door was closed so I knocked and waited.

'Come in,' said a voice.

I entered the room and saw Joseph sitting behind a desk.

'Good evening, sir,' he said. 'Take a seat please.'

19

There was a long pause after I'd sat down during which my hopes and aspirations began rapidly to fade. The last time I'd seen Joseph was when he was running into the shadows having just accused me of treachery. Now, it seemed, my fate was in his hands. I bowed to the inevitable and awaited his verdict.

'I would like to begin, sir,' he said, 'by apologising on behalf of myself and my colleagues Matthew and Thomas. We entirely misunderstood your intentions when you brought us here and we wrongfully denounced you for betraying us. Again I apologise because actually you were doing us an inestimable favour. Through your guidance we have shed off the burdens of physical toil and are now very well-placed in respectable employment. For this I wish not only to apologise but also to thank you.'

'Think nothing of it,' I said.

Joseph rocked his head from side to side.

'Now,' he said, taking a deep breath, 'I must tell you that a certain person within the agency takes a very dim view of your application.'

'I suppose you mean Johnson.'

'Correct.'

'I see.'

'He claims that your qualifications are limited and your motivations entirely selfish. He's all for stamping the word REJECT on your file in red letters before your case is even heard.'

'Rather peremptory,' I said.

'Which is why Matthew, Thomas and I have intervened,' said Joseph. 'We have overruled him.'

'But isn't he in charge of you?'

'Why should he be?'

'I just assumed he was.'

'Well, he isn't.'

'Oh, sorry.'

Joseph smiled in a beneficent manner.

'No need to apologise, sir,' he said. 'It is a common assumption that people like us are naturally the underlings: that we're only capable of working in car washes, oil drum yards or tyre fitting depots. We have learnt to accept this outlook but fortunately there are a few enlightened individuals like yourself who treat us as equals.'

'Is that why you intervened?' I asked.

'No,' Joseph replied. 'We intervened because you still owe us last week's productivity bonus.'

'Ah.'

'It's in our interests as well as yours to get you through this registration process as swiftly as possible.'

'Yes, I imagine it is.'

He adopted a businesslike tone of voice.

'Now as you probably know,' he said, 'this is a Stage Two facility. All the conventional preliminaries have been eliminated to allow applicants to be 'fast-tracked' through the system. This can be achieved in less than an hour.'

'Sounds impressive,' I said.

'Obviously there's an alternative. Anyone is free to choose the traditional Stage One process but I should warn you that it's very slow and cumbersome and involves all kinds of personal intrusion. It also entails indefinite internment in one of our dormitory blocks. Undoubtedly not to be recommended.'

'It's alright,' I said. 'You've already persuaded me. I'll opt for Stage Two.'

'Good,' said Joseph. 'Just sign this please, sir.'

He slid a sheet of typewritten paper across the desk towards me.

'What is it?' I asked.

'Simply a statement declaring that you are willing to be deported.'

'But that defeats the object!' I protested.

I began to rise from my seat but Joseph waved his hand and gently urged me to sit down again.

'Don't be concerned, sir,' he said. 'You're forgetting what country you are in. The language employed here is deliberately abstruse. There's a subtle difference between what a word suggests and what it actually means. 'Willingness' doesn't carry any sort of legal weight. It's just a term of convenience to satisfy the general public. This in turn satisfies the authorities. Believe me, once you've signed the form they'll forget all about you.'

He leaned towards me and spoke in a confidential tone.

'Matthew, Thomas and myself have all signed it.'

'Really?' I said with astonishment.

'Of course,' he said. 'As I've told you many times before: we are very flexible.'

Just as Joseph had promised, the registration process was completed in less than an hour. After I'd signed my statement he went to a machine and made several copies. These he placed carefully in a filing cabinet. I expected him to give me a copy but he didn't. He merely returned to his desk and smiled.

'I suppose I'll be issued with some kind of identity card?' I ventured.

'Oh, no,' he said. 'This country doesn't believe in identity cards.'

'Why is that then?'

'They're regarded as an infringement of liberty.'

'Well, how will I be able to prove I've registered?'

Joseph shrugged.

'That's a question I haven't been asked before,' he said. 'I'm afraid you'll just have to put your faith in the system.'

He then sent me through to an adjoining room where Matthew was sitting behind a mesh window. It transpired that I was entitled to a one-off cash payment to help me with my travel expenses. Once I'd received it he directed me onward to a hospitality suite. Here I was given a light meal together with a soft drink. Sitting at a neighbouring table was the man in the yellow and green boiler suit. There was no sign, however, of the two sulky women and the other three men.

The main exit was clearly marked but before I departed I wanted to see Joseph again. I now had enough money to pay him and his companions their productivity bonus. Under the circumstances I thought it was the least I could do. Frustratingly, though, when I attempted to go back through the building the way I'd come, I found the doors inaccessible. There was nobody to ask so eventually I concluded that I would have to try and catch them another time. I headed for the exit and a few minutes later I walked out of the gate and onto the main road.

High above me loomed the familiar railway arch. For a few seconds I stood in the darkness contemplating the long walk back to the cafe. There was no traffic but parked in the lay-by was a solitary vehicle that I instantly recognised as Tamara's dormobile. All its lights were on and its engine was running. Attached to the rear was a large placard that said:

FREE HARCOURT NOW!

Tamara was sitting in the driver's seat reading a book so I walked over and tapped on the glass. She peered out at me before winding down the window.

'It's not very good for the environment,' I said, by way of greeting, 'running the engine like that.'

'What do you care about the environment?' she replied. 'In fact, what do you care about anything?'

'Whoah, steady,' I said. 'I was only making a friendly observation.'

'Well, I'm not in the mood for 'friendly observations',' she said. 'Life's been very fraught lately.'

'Why, what's the matter?'

'Haven't you heard? They've interned Harcourt. He's in there at this very moment!'

She pointed an accusing finger towards the reception centre.

'What's he done then?' I asked.

'It's what he hasn't done that's more important. He refused on principle to be fast-tracked and now he's being detained at their pleasure.'

'Well, that could be an indefinite term.'

'I'm fully aware of that!'

Tamara glared at me as though it was all my fault. Privately I wondered why Harcourt hadn't simply signed the declaration and saved himself a lot of hardship. I knew, however, that it would be a waste of time voicing my inner thoughts to Tamara. She plainly wanted a martyr and Harcourt fitted the bill perfectly.

'What's happening at the protest camp?' I enquired.

'It's all collapsed,' she said. 'They couldn't go on without Harcourt's leadership.'

'And the strike?'

'Still in deadlock.'

Tamara got out of the dormobile and did a few stretches at the roadside. Then she turned to me.

'I see you managed to walk out of the place unimpeded,' she remarked. 'I presume you were fast-tracked?'

'Yes,' I admitted.

She sighed and shook her head.

'Well, I'm not really inclined to offer you a lift,' she said, 'but I'm finished here for the evening and there's a seat in the front if you want it.'

'How about a contribution towards your petrol?' I said.

'Forget it.'

Without a further word she returned to the driver's seat while I climbed in at the passenger side. She drove off at her usual breakneck speed and as we whizzed along I enquired whether she knew what had become of Kingsnorth.

'He's given up and gone home,' said Tamara. 'He realised this country was beyond redemption so he and a few others repaired the boat and sailed away.'

'You mean other people from the protest camp?'

'Yes.'

As I absorbed the news I realised that my last link with my former life had been broken.

'I had a quarter share in that boat,' I said.

'Well,' replied Tamara, 'you'd better send them an invoice then, hadn't you?'

In due course we neared the cafe.

'Could you drop me here please?' I said.

Tamara pulled up and I thanked her for the ride.

'See you around,' she said, before driving away.

The hour was now very late but the lights in the flat were still on. I delved in my pocket and found my key. When I entered Eva was waiting for me.

'Who was that who dropped you off?' she asked.

Apparently she'd been watching at the window.

'Tamara,' I said. 'You know her: she collects glasses some evenings at The Wheatsheaf.'

'Oh, that busybody,' said Eva.

'Er…yes.'

'I wish she'd stop interfering in other people's lives. Always pursuing some righteous cause or other. She was going around the pub the other night trying to get all the customers to sign a petition.'

'What about?'

'I don't know and I don't care. Norman got quite cross with her. He explained that they're not interested in petitions and protests and what have you. All they're bothered about is their beer.'

'And their quiz,' I added.

'Yes, well, that too,' Eva conceded.

She handed me an envelope.

'By the way,' she said. 'This came for you.'

Inside the envelope was an application form for the new government agency.

'I wonder why they've sent me this,' I said.

'I requested it on your behalf,' said Eva, 'to save you the trouble.'

'But I'm not interested in joining.'

'Yes, you are,' she said. 'You just won't admit it.'

With a show of indignation I had a look through the form. I expected to be deluged with countless questions about my background, my education, my country of origin and so forth. Instead, there were just a few simple boxes to tick.

'They seem to have set the bar very low,' I observed. 'Virtually anyone could apply.'

'Well, the reason's obvious,' said Eva.

'Is it?'

'It means they'll have more taxpayers.'

'Oh, yes, I suppose so.'

'More taxes to pay for roads, railways, schools, hospitals, libraries and public transport.'

'Or for building more reception centres.'

'Precisely,' said Eva. 'It's self-perpetuating.'

I folded the form and put it in my inside pocket.

'Perhaps that's for the future,' I said. 'In the meantime I've got to think about work tomorrow.'

'At the car wash?'

'Of course.'

I explained that I no longer had a van.

'I'll have to walk all the way there,' I said. 'I suppose you couldn't open the cafe early so I can have breakfast before I leave?'

'No,' said Eva.

'Thought not.'

'And don't forget you're still overdue with your rent.'

'Aha!'

In a twinkling I produced the cash I'd been given for travel expenses. I'd originally intended to set it aside so that I could pay Joseph, Matthew and Thomas their productivity bonus.

Now, though, I reformulated the plan. My priority was keeping Eva mollified: therefore, I immediately handed over what I owed her for the rent. After lengthy negotiations she then accompanied me to the cafe kitchen so that I could make myself some sandwiches. (She charged me for the ingredients but allowed me ten percent discount because I was a regular customer.)

20

When I set off for work next morning I soon discovered I wasn't the only early riser. Dozens of liveried minibuses went past on the main road full of hotel workers, airport baggage handlers and car park attendants, all predestined for another thankless day. In every lay-by, meanwhile, stood small groups of men waiting to be picked up by vans. (There were further pre-arranged collection points on petrol station forecourts and outside 24-hour burger bars.) Many vans bore the company names of builders, plumbers, joiners, electricians and countless other trades. Some vans provided particular services advertised in bold letters on their side panels: windscreen replacement, for example, or sewage pumping. The majority of vans, however, were unadorned and (chiefly) white. What they all had in common was their relentless hurry to get to wherever they were going. As they approached a pickup point they would bib their horns and flash their headlights and then come speeding up, the doors would be thrown open allowing the workers to pile inside before they zoomed away again.

All this frantic scurrying around was monitored by the occupants of another type of van: the unmarked grey vans of the new government agency. They waited at strategic locations watching all the comings and goings and presumably keeping an eye open for unregistered persons. I felt rather conspicuous whenever I walked past such a van. Joseph had assured me I need not worry but even so it was a bit of a strain. There was simply no denying the fact that I was a cash-in-hand worker paying no tax. My pale blue overalls (with a silver streak) were no real proof of authenticity and strictly speaking I should have been a prime target.

As I reflected on my precarious situation I suddenly remembered the application form in my inside pocket. It struck me that it would do no harm if I ticked the boxes and popped it into a post box. The only problem was that I didn't have a pen (the form specified black ink for filling it in). Just then I saw a grey van parked at the roadside just ahead of me. There were three uniformed men sitting side-by-side in the front. On the spur of the moment I decided that openness was the best policy so I approached the van and tapped on the window. At the same instant I realised it was the men who'd picked me up the day before. The one nearest the window peered out at me and then wound it down.

'Yes?'

'Sorry to bother you,' I said, 'but have you got a black pen I could borrow for a minute?'

After a brief delay he handed me a pen. I thanked him before walking over to a nearby bench where I sat down and began filling in the form. While I did so I became aware of being watched from the van. I completed the form, signed it and sealed it in the pre-paid envelope. Then I returned to the van.

'Thanks,' I said again.

The man took his pen back.

'Haven't I seen you before?' he enquired.

'Yes,' I replied. 'We met yesterday at a car wash.'

'Oh, that's right,' he said. 'Get registered okay?'

His tone was much less brusque than the day before: in fact it could almost be described as friendly.

'Yes, thanks,' I said, 'though obviously I can't prove it.'

'Well, we can take you in again if you like.'

I looked at him with surprise.

'You mean go and register again?'

'Yes.'

'Why would I want to do that?'

'So that you can reclaim your travel expenses,' he said. 'We've got a few regulars who do it all the time.'

'But don't they get recognised?'

'Doesn't matter if they do.'

Now his colleague in the adjoining seat entered the conversation.

'We're expected to take in a fixed quota of people every day,' he explained. 'The quicker we take them in the sooner we can finish work.'

'Oh. I see.'

'So if you came with us you'd actually be doing us a favour.'

I had to admit that the money I'd been given for travel expenses was quite generous. After all, I'd managed to pay a week's rent out of it. Nevertheless I was reluctant to abuse the system.

'Thanks all the same,' I said, 'but I'll give it a miss if you don't mind.'

'Fair enough,' said the man by the window. 'We just thought we'd mention it.'

The driver leant over.

'It's time we moved,' he said. 'Can we give you a lift somewhere?'

'Well, I'm due at the car wash at eight o'clock,' I replied. 'I'm not late but it's rather a long way.'

'Hop in the back.'

When I opened the door I was astonished to see the two sulky women sitting in the gloomy interior. I slammed the door behind me and we were soon moving away. After I'd settled in I made an attempt to talk to the women but they made it clear they weren't interested. Throughout the journey they complained to one another in their usual whining tones and I concluded that this was how they talked all the time.

A mere quarter of an hour later we pulled up outside the car wash and the driver let me out. After he'd shut the door I asked him about the women.

'Are those two of your regulars?'

'Yes,' he said, 'but they're pushing their luck a bit.'

'Oh, yes?'

'To our knowledge it's at least their fifth time around.'

The two of us shook hands and said goodbye and the van continued on its way. It was now twenty minutes to eight. The gates to the car wash were closed. Having arrived early for work I still had a bit of time to kill so I walked up the road to the parade of shops and posted my application form. No sooner had I dropped it into the postbox, however, than I began debating whether I'd chosen the correct course. Was it really the ideal job for me? My observations of recent days had made it plain that the new government agency was no more than a sham. I'd seen for myself that the Stage 2 process was riddled with all sorts of loopholes and ambiguities. Evidently the authorities had bent over backwards to try and provide a human touch. They'd spent a fortune on a state-of-the-art reception centre with its fresh paint, its tea trolley and its hospitality suite but it had swiftly metamorphosed into a merry-go-round. Admittedly there was a high-profile 'guest' currently languishing within its bounds but he was the exception rather than the rule. Harcourt had been made a scapegoat because he'd insisted on entering the country through the proper channels. He'd only come here in the first place to try and help cure the people of their woes and rather ungratefully they'd rejected his overtures. Nonetheless his sojourn was likely to be short-lived. There was no doubt Tamara would kick up such a fuss that ultimately they'd let him go just to keep her quiet.

And this was the key to their problem: I'd learnt since I'd been here that what they liked least of all in this country was a fuss. Consequently the Stage 2 process was doomed to failure.

To succeed properly it would require some ruthless individual to give it a thorough shake-up. They would have to instigate a strict programme whereby all unregistered persons were herded into reception centres and their credentials properly examined. Failure to comply would automatically trigger indefinite internment. There would be no friendly ladies with tea trolleys, no hospitality suite and categorically no allowances for travel expenses.

Meanwhile a surveillance operation would be conducted to track down tradesmen who employed unregistered labour. They, in turn, would then be subject to sanctions. Only under these harsh conditions could the Stage 2 process fulfil its original purpose.

That was the theory anyway. Obviously the practical application of such draconian measures was unthinkable in a so-called progressive society. It would cause more than a mere fuss: there'd be a public outcry! Howls of protest! Nobody would want to have anything to do with it.

Especially not me.

With these thoughts in mind I wandered back to the car wash to begin my day's work. It was now eight o'clock but to my surprise I found the gates still closed. Normally I would have expected Kevin and the others to have turned up bright and early and start getting the equipment ready. This morning, though, there was no activity whatsoever. I then remembered that I still had my own key to the yard so I swung open the gates and went inside. To my horror I was confronted by a complete mess. When I'd been in charge I'd always ensured the place was left tidy overnight. I saw to it that the jet wash was replenished with soap for the following day, that the hose was neatly coiled up and that all the sponges and cloths were stowed on their respective racks. Likewise the vacuum cleaner was unplugged and the waste container emptied. The general idea was to make the business look presentable to prospective customers but actually none of this had been done. Kevin and the others appeared to have simply abandoned the yard the previous evening and gone home. They hadn't even bothered to sweep up! There were huge puddles everywhere and I saw at once that the main drain cover was blocked with detritus.

By now the first customer of the day had arrived. It was a woman. I apologised for the delay and urged her to avoid the puddles when she got out of her car. She was smartly dressed and carrying a briefcase.

'Full wash and valet service?' I enquired.

'Well, yes,' she said, 'I suppose I might as well have it cleaned while I'm here.'

I thought this was an odd thing to say but I didn't question the remark. Instead, I led her across the yard to the office.

'You can wait in here if you like,' I said. 'We're planning to provide customers with complimentary coffee and pastries but we haven't got around to it yet.'

'Thank you.'

I unlocked the door and she went inside. At the same moment I noticed that the ledger had been carelessly left lying on the desk instead of being tucked away in the drawer. There were also some scraps of paper with figures written on them. The woman sat down and immediately pulled the ledger towards her. She then took some reading glasses out of her pocket, put them on and began leafing through the pages. I watched her with mild fascination, pondering whether to challenge her or not. After a few seconds she looked up and saw that I was still standing there. She examined me inquisitorially over the rim of her glasses.

'Yes?'

'Er…sorry,' I said. 'Nothing.'

I then withdrew from her presence.

I'd just finished jet washing her car and was about to start vacuum cleaning when Kevin and Pete's van pulled hurriedly into the yard. I wasn't sure whether they were expecting me or not but actually they seemed highly pleased to see me.

'Good job you're here,' said Kevin. 'Those other cunts have let us down badly.'

'You mean Dave, Gaz and Kenny?' I asked.

'Yes,' he said. 'We waited on the ring road for half an hour and they never turned up.'

'Cunts,' said Pete.

Kevin glanced at the car I was working on and then gazed around the yard.

'Where's the customer gone?'

'I let her wait in the office,' I said. 'I thought it would be a nice gesture.'

He nodded thoughtfully.

'Good idea,' he said. 'What we really ought to do in future is offer complimentary coffee and pastries.'

Another car had just entered the yard so Kevin went to deal with them while Pete took over the vacuum cleaner. In the meantime I went across to the drain cover and swept away the detritus. Soon the puddles were much smaller, then the sun came out and the yard began to regain a semblance of normality. Despite their rather rough edges I got on fairly well with Kevin and Pete and enjoyed working alongside them. I grabbed a cloth and began polishing windscreens, headlights and hub caps. By this time Kevin was jet washing the second car which meant the first one would soon need moving out of the way.

'Did you say it was a lady driver?' Pete asked.

'Yes,' I said.

'Right. I'll pop over and tell her it's ready.'

There was a spring in his step as he approached the office. He was whistling a jolly tune but the whistling abruptly ceased when he glimpsed through the window. I saw him stiffen slightly before gently knocking on the door and putting his head inside. He exchanged a few words with the woman and then a few more after that. Finally he went in and closed the door behind him. By this time Kevin had begun to peer cautiously across the yard towards the office. There was a further delay and then Pete emerged and trudged through the remains of the puddles towards Kevin. They conferred for a few moments and then came over to me. I noticed they both had a very subdued look about them.

'You didn't tell me that was Gillian Twigg in there,' Pete murmured.

'Is she Bob's wife?'

'Yes.'

'Sorry,' I said. 'I've never met her before.'

'She's been going through the ledger,' said Kevin. 'She's an accountant. She takes care of Bob's finances and now she's doing Ted Gresham's as well.'

'She can appraise an entire balance sheet at a glance,' said Pete, 'so she'll make short work of our ledger.'

I didn't mention the discrepancies I'd spotted the other day. There was no need. Kevin and Pete clearly knew that their fiddle was about to be detected.

'What are you going to do?' I asked.

'Not sure yet,' said Kevin.

There was little more to discuss. A third customer was now waiting to be attended to so Kevin and Pete swiftly returned to their work stations. I moved Gillian Twigg's car out of the way and took her keys over to the office. She was just placing some handwritten notes in her briefcase.

'Your car's ready,' I said.

'Thanks,' she said. 'How much do I owe you?'

I told her the amount and she paid in cash. There was no tip. She then watched as I entered the amount in the ledger (along with the time and date).

'You're in charge of the books, are you?' she enquired.

'Well, I was until a few days ago but then Kevin took over.'

'I see.'

A movement outside the window caught my eye and I saw that both Kevin and Pete were frantically applying an extra coat of polish to her car. They rubbed and rubbed as though their futures depended on it. By the time they'd finished they must have expended at least half a bottle of polish. Meanwhile a queue of other customers waited patiently in the background.

'I'd better get back to work,' I said. 'We're a bit short-staffed today.'

'Yes,' she said, 'so I see.'

She gave me a smile and went outside to her shining car. Pete held the door open for her as she got in and Kevin voiced some pleasantry. A few moments later she drove away. There was no opportunity for a post-mortem because we now had a considerable backlog of other vehicles to clear. I could tell from their body language, however, that my two workmates were deeply concerned. On several occasions during the morning I saw them murmuring to one another with their heads together. Additional cars were constantly arriving which kept us all busy but I had no doubt the pair of them were hatching some plan. They kept well away from the office and took no part in any cash transactions. Kevin was still nominally in charge, though, and at lunchtime he announced that he was just going out to get some fish and chips.

'Plaice or cod?' he enquired.

'Plaice, please,' I said. 'I'll give you the money in advance if you like.'

I proffered my few remaining coins but he was reluctant to take them.

'No, don't worry about that,' he said with a wave of his hand. 'We can settle up later.'

He began sauntering towards his van.

'I think I'll go along for the ride,' said Pete nonchalantly.

At that moment we were making the most of a quiet spell after a particularly frenetic period. There was only one car waiting to be polished so I had no objection to 'minding the shop' while the two of them went on their errand. Kevin bibbed his horn as they drove out of the yard and then they were gone. Ten minutes later another car arrived which meant I had to single-handedly operate the jet wash and the vacuum cleaner and then do yet more polishing. A further twenty minutes past. By this time Kevin and Pete should have returned but actually there was no sign of them. I continued working and resigned myself to going without plaice and chips. Fortunately I still had a few sandwiches remaining but even so the situation was a little worrying. The afternoon rush was imminent and I was just beginning to wonder how I would cope on my own when Ted Gresham's car suddenly pulled in through the gates. He parked in a corner and when he got out I saw that he was wearing pale blue overalls with a silver streak. Immediately he came marching over, seized a sponge and began working vigorously alongside me. For the next two hours he never uttered a word as we serviced a succession of cars. It was now patently obvious that Kevin and Pete weren't coming back but somehow we managed to keep on top of it all. As a matter of fact in terms of productivity we did fairly well considering there were only two of us. Not until almost dusk did the feverish activity cease. As the last car departed Ted closed the gates behind it before heading into the office and switching the lights on.

A few minutes later he invited me to join him. When I peered through the doorway he was sitting at the desk examining the ledger.

'You'll definitely be coming to work tomorrow, won't you?' he enquired.

'Of course,' I said.

'The reason I ask is because it's getting more and more difficult to find dependable people.'

'Yes, so I gather.'

'What happened to those three fellows who liked saying their prayers?'

'They enrolled with the new government agency.'

Ted nodded reflectively as he absorbed the news.

'Don't blame them at all,' he said. 'From what I've heard it's easy money.'

Lying on the desk beside the ledger was a pile of banknotes comprising the afternoon's takings. Ted now counted them and gave half to me.

'Thanks,' I said. 'What are you going to do about recruitment?'

'I'll have to have a think about it overnight,' he replied, 'but obviously you'll be in charge from now on.'

After we'd given the yard a quick tidy-up Ted offered me a lift home in his car. Half an hour later he dropped me off at the cafe and said he'd pick me up at seven thirty the following morning. The cafe lights were still on so I went in and found Eva alone again (the owner had gone to the cash-and-carry to stock up). I told her about my day at the car wash and then presented her with a week's rent in advance. There was also enough money for a substantial meal. Eventually she closed the cafe. We went up to the flat and then she asked if I was going to The Wheatsheaf.

'It depends,' I said. 'Are you working there tonight?'

'No,' she answered. 'It's my evening off.'

'I don't have to go if you don't want me to.'

'Then don't.'

21

Next day I awoke bright and early and enjoyed a leisurely breakfast in the cafe. At seven thirty I said goodbye to Eva before going outside to wait for Ted Gresham to arrive. I was wearing my pale blue overalls with a silver streak and I made a mental note that I really should take them to the laundromat very soon. Now that I was back in charge of the car wash it was imperative that I looked smart and presentable.

When a quarter of an hour had passed I began to wonder why Ted was late. I knew from experience that he was a stickler for punctuality so I guessed he'd probably been held up on some urgent business matter. Or maybe he had a puncture. Or perhaps he was caught in a traffic jam. Whatever the reason I had no choice but to continue waiting for him.

At eight o'clock Eva kindly brought me out a cup of coffee with a lid on it.

'I saw you standing here looking all forlorn,' she said. 'I thought it might cheer you up a bit.'

Her gesture reminded me that I really ought to mention to Ted my idea about complimentary coffee and pastries. I also had in mind a few other improvements to the car wash (better signage and so forth). I was optimistic we'd be able to implement them in due course.

For the time being, however, there was still no sign of Ted.

Fifteen minutes later a grey van pulled up beside me. There were three uniformed men sitting in the front. The man nearest the window wound it down and asked me my name. I told him and he consulted a sheet of paper.

'Yes, it's you we're looking for,' he said. 'I'm pleased to inform you that your application has been accepted.'

'That was quick,' I said.

'Well, we've had a bit of a shake-up just lately: we're much more efficient than before.'

He directed me to 'hop in'. When I opened the back door and looked inside I discovered that I had two fellow passengers. It was the sulky women. They said nothing when I joined them so I didn't attempt to make any conversation. I slammed the door shut and the journey resumed. During the next half hour I

occasionally peeped through the observation window and swiftly established that we were heading for the reception centre. As we drew near our destination I saw that the sign outside had been altered slightly. It now said:
NATIONAL RECEPTION AND PROCESSING CENTRE
STAGE THREE

The van turned in through the gateway and halted. Somebody opened the back door and immediately the two sulky women got out and began ambling towards building A. To their evident surprise, however, they were ordered by the men from the van to accompany them towards a building with the letter X stencilled on its door. I could still hear their whining voices as they vanished inside. Meanwhile, another man appeared in the doorway of building A and beckoned me to join him. I recognised him at once as the man who'd lent me his black pen.

'Welcome to Stage Three,' he said. 'You'll probably notice a few changes around here.'

'More than a few,' I remarked.

'Yes, well, we've had a bit of a shake-up just lately: we're much more efficient than before.'

Outside the door was a yellow refuse skip containing about half a dozen upturned tea trolleys.

'Does that mean no more tea and biscuits?' I enquired.

'I'm afraid so,' he said. 'No more friendly ladies serving tea and biscuits, no more hospitality suite and categorically no more payments for travel expenses.'

He stood holding the door open for me to enter.

I peered around and tried without success to imagine the days when this place was a funfair.

'Just out of interest,' I asked, 'who's in charge now?'

'I think you know him,' came the reply. 'His name's Johnson.'

Printed in Great Britain
by Amazon